"We're driving around until they're finished with the first witness." Delaney looked over her shoulder at Bruce for a split second.

His heart sped up as the mail truck sped down the parking ramps. *Let this time be different.*

A shot rang out. People screamed on the courthouse steps and uniformed men ran out, looking up, weapons in hand. A metal crunching sound reverberated through the vehicle. Bruce reeled forward as the truck spun backward. Someone honked.

"Have we been hit?"

"Everyone okay?" Delaney shouted at the same time.

So the truck had been shot at, but he didn't see where the bullet had landed. Bruce launched himself out of his seat and sat next to Winnie, both shielding her and frantically checking for any injuries.

Delaney picked up her radio and spoke rapidly. "Shots fired. Two down."

Bruce groaned, hung his head and kissed Winnie's forehead.

Someone had been waiting for them.

Heather Woodhaven earned her pilot's license, rode a hot-air balloon over the safari lands of Kenya, parasailed over Caribbean seas, lived through an accidental detour onto a black-diamond ski trail in Aspen and snorkeled among stingrays before becoming a mother of three and wife of one. She channels her love for adventure into writing characters who find themselves in extraordinary circumstances.

Books by Heather Woodhaven

Love Inspired Suspense

PROTECTED SECRETS

HEATHER WOODHAVEN

HARLEQUIN® LOVE INSPIRED® SUSPENSE

Recycling programs
for this product may
not exist in your area.

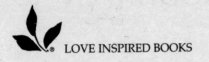

LOVE INSPIRED BOOKS

ISBN-13: 978-1-335-49055-1

Protected Secrets

Copyright © 2018 by Heather Humrichouse

www.Harlequin.com

Printed in U.S.A.

Not that we are sufficient of ourselves to think any thing as of ourselves; but our sufficiency is of God.

—2 Corinthians 3:5

For my children and nieces and nephews. Thanks for all the laughs and stories and imaginative playtime throughout the years. You guys rock.

ONE

Bruce Walker recognized his assistant as the only other person in the parking lot. Her silver curls and thick glasses reflected the sun cresting over the tall trees in the distance. "I owe you big, Nancy." He approached, holding two to-go cups. "I know Saturday mornings are precious."

"Just missing my cartoons." She paused. "You see, it used to be Saturday mornings when the cartoons—"

"I'm not *that* young, Nancy."

She accepted the coffee with a wink. "Where's your little darling? I thought you might bring her with you."

Aside from Nancy King's attention for detail and unmatched work ethic, she acted as an honorary grandmother to his two-year-old daughter. It was a much-needed connection that he appreciated as a single dad. "She's at a friend's house this morning, which is why I'm taking advantage of your time. I feel like we're not quite ready for the big sales pitch Monday."

Ever since Trevor, his stepbrother, quit the company six months ago, Bruce had yet to fill the gaping hole Trevor had left as his former partner. Nancy crossed the parking lot with him. He entered the code to momentarily disarm the security system and unlocked the door.

On weekends, there was usually only one security guard on duty. At that moment, Max rounded the corner, hair freshly buzzed in a military cut he'd likely been wearing for over forty years. Aside from his uniform of an ironed white shirt and navy pants, he wore a holster with a gun and Taser. It seemed like overkill to Bruce, but he relied on the expertise of the security firm to make those decisions. "How's it going this morning, Max?"

"Before you came, it was quiet on all fronts, just how I like it." Max whistled as he strode past them. For good measure, Max checked the locks on the door they'd entered before he rounded the next corner.

Bruce's phone dinged with an alert: Network Down. He groaned. There was no explanation for that, but it didn't necessarily mean the problem was on their end. "Slight change of plans, Nancy. I'm going to need to make a quick stop in the server room to make sure everything is okay."

She matched his stride. "Can I do anything?"

"I'll need to talk with someone in the IT department first. I think Doug is on call today. Could you text him? He should've received the same alert I did." He shoved the stairwell door open since the elevator worked at a snail's pace.

Nancy didn't complain. He heard her steps behind him until he reached the basement level when her phone dinged. "Doug says it's just come back online, but he doesn't know why the blip occurred in the first place."

So it could've been a connectivity glitch. "Tell him that since I'm here I'm going to take a look and call him back in a minute." He stepped out into the open area filled with cubicles. "Nancy, you can wait for me in my office if you want."

In his peripheral vision, he caught sight of someone disappearing behind a cubicle wall. He froze for half a second, caught off guard. It was possible his eyes were playing tricks on him. Glad Nancy hadn't left yet, he turned his head and said in low tones, "Send Max a text and tell him to make his rounds down here now."

Her eyebrows rose, but she didn't argue. Her thumbs flew over her phone's keypad.

A blip of light flashed from the cubicle to his left. Bruce strained his neck and saw a computer monitor on with a script shooting lines of code out faster than he could read. So he wasn't imagining things. Someone else *was* down here. "Hello?" he called out.

No one spoke, but his neck tingled. If someone had come in through the front doors, Max would've noticed. The man always double-checked doors were locked after someone entered, and the security key code would've alerted him to their presence. So who was here? How had they gotten in?

And what had they come here to do?

Bruce took a step toward the computer screen and tried to read the script.

"What's going on?" Nancy stood to his right and looked down.

His stomach turned to lead. An unsanctioned update was uploading to all the bank systems that subscribed to their risk-analysis software. Bruce set down his coffee, leaned over and entered the administrator commands necessary to quit the process.

"I wouldn't do that if I were you." A voice reverberated through the room.

Bruce straightened. Nancy's face blanched and coffee ran down her wrist and dripped onto the blue carpet. A man—short in stature, wearing a black T-shirt and jeans—held a gun in his shaking hand.

Once Bruce managed to move his focus from the gun to the man's face, he recognized Andy Williamson, one of his data analysts. Andy narrowed his eyes and steadied his aim on Bruce. "Move away from the computer."

He did, using the opportunity to slide in front of Nancy. "Andy, what are you doing? Put the gun down." Bruce put one hand behind him and gestured for Nancy to get down. Instead, he felt her shaking fingers grip the back of his shirt. She tugged him backward. No doubt she felt some maternal instinct toward him, but there was no time to argue about who should save whom.

"Don't take another step," Andy barked.

The tugging on the back of his shirt stopped. Bruce didn't know Andy as well as he did some of the other employees, but he'd seemed friendly. Maybe there was some sort of stress in his life that had made him snap. If he was a reasonable man, there was hope he could be talked down. "Andy, I can help you. Just put—"

"You weren't supposed to be here. If you'd just stayed away you never would've known."

"Known what?" Bruce asked. "What are you trying to do?"

Andy raked his free hand down the side of his face but his weapon stayed trained on Bruce. "You need to turn around and walk away now. Don't interfere and forget you ever saw a thing, for your own good. You don't mess with the—"

The stairwell door at the opposite end of the floor

opened. Max was coming. Bruce couldn't let him walk into an ambush. "Gun!"

As Andy spun around, Bruce clutched Nancy's wrist and pulled her downward into a crouch as he ran the two of them past the cubicles.

A trio of gunshots rang out.

He felt Nancy flinch at each ping of the bullets. Bruce looked over his shoulder just in time to see Max crumple to the ground.

"No!" A sob escaped Nancy's lips.

Bruce pulled her around the corner to a darkened hallway. "Follow me."

He ran to the nearest door and placed his hand on the biometric scanner. Two beeps sounded, followed by a click. He wrenched open the door as Andy rounded the hallway corner.

Bruce gave Nancy a gentle push so she'd step inside the server room first. Then he met Andy's anguished but determined gaze as Andy raised the handgun. Bruce ducked behind the fireproof door and the bullets hit the steel in front of him. He pulled on the handle of the hydraulic door so it would close before Andy reached them. "Come on, come on, come on." The lock clicked, but he had a hard time letting go of the handle.

"Won't he be able to get in, too?"

"No."

"But we're trapped." Nancy's voice shook. She didn't wait for him to answer and held the phone to her ear. "Gunman shooting at us." She rattled the address to what had to be police dispatch and stepped into the small space between the servers and the wall before sinking down to the ground.

Bruce forced his fingers to relax and let go of the handle. He took one step back and watched the door. He stood inside the most secure room in the building, designed to withstand most hackers and thieves, but he didn't remember "bulletproof" as being one of the selling points. The steel seemed to be holding up for now.

At least Andy, as an analyst, didn't have credentials to enter the server room. Bruce pulled out a keyboard from one of the racks and typed in the commands to shut down the outgoing update in midstream. He then turned off the network completely so Andy couldn't try again.

Their company provided risk-analysis software to 30 percent of the banks in the country. If Andy had been able to sneak malware in with an update, it was impossible to guess just how much damage he could've done both to the banks and to his company's reputation.

Another gunshot sounded. Bruce recoiled, remembering Max's crumpled body out there. He couldn't afford to think about him right now because Andy wasn't giving up. Unless Nancy had a gun in her purse, he had no options for weapons. The room only contained racks of servers. Nancy's hand reached up in the air. "We need to pray," she whispered.

He stared at her hand for a moment before realizing she was right. There was nothing else left for him to do. Bruce accepted her shaking fingers and sank to the floor. Nancy murmured pleas for protection and help so fast his brain couldn't register everything she said. *I agree, Lord.* It was the only prayer he could manage. At a moment like this, all he could think about was his daughter. Would she lose the only parent who wanted her?

The police couldn't come fast enough.

* * *

Delaney Patton had joined the US Marshals almost three years ago to run from her mistakes. She didn't think she'd be sent right back to face the past.

The rental car idled while she stared at the nondescript blue house she'd once called home in Ames, Iowa. Later, it was the place where she'd gotten the news that her boyfriend, and fellow police officer, had died. The police chief had told her while she'd fought to keep a brave face. She hadn't been strong enough. She'd broken down, and then her water had broken.

Most days, the memories didn't feel real, more like recalling a bad dream. Early labor had followed the tragic news, and in her grief and despair, she'd decided to give the baby up for adoption. Her little girl deserved better than a single mom who couldn't cope.

Delaney sucked in a sharp breath. Her appearance still looked relatively the same—long brunette hair always pulled back in a ponytail—but she was a different person now. If given the opportunity to do it all over again, she wouldn't make the same choices. But life didn't offer do-overs.

It did no good to wallow. The Marshals had transferred her back to the Southern District of Iowa because Delaney knew it like the back of her hand. And while the base of operations was located in Des Moines, it was possible she'd be sent to Ames occasionally.

Delaney shifted the car into Drive. She'd found out what she needed to know. She could handle being in Ames, even on this street, without breaking down. Now she just had to work up the courage to let her parents know she was back in the state.

Her phone rang. "US Marshals. Deputy Marshal Patton."

"Welcome home!" The deep boisterous voice could only belong to her previous police chief, Stephen Bradford, now the newly appointed US marshal for the Southern District of Idaho.

"Thank you, sir." She tried to sound enthusiastic, but it fell flat. It was hard to shake the feeling that her new boss knew too much about her. He had, after all, been the one to hold her as she'd cried all the way to the hospital.

"Listen, I know you just flew in last night. I wanted to give you the weekend to get settled but—"

"Urgent case?" Hope blossomed. Going after a fugitive case that would take her across the state sounded like the perfect transition to the district.

"It's an expedited protection custody assignment. The Bureau pushed it through to the US Attorney's Office this afternoon."

Delaney felt her eyebrows rise. Normal procedure took at least ten business days to get witness protection from the Marshals. To have it scheduled within one day meant something big had happened. "Any details?"

"They're coming to me piecemeal. Two witnesses stopped a hacker from planting a back door that would provide access to bank credentials. The hacker allegedly murdered the security guard and escaped before law enforcement arrived on the scene. Security cameras and access logs had been disabled. No murder weapon has been found."

"The hacker?" Delaney tried to make sense of what she was hearing. The situation was certainly serious, but so far she didn't see the reason for expedited protection.

"Arrested an hour ago. Feds think he's the key to bringing down the CryptTakers."

That particular criminal organization had been wreaking havoc across the country for the past three years. Last year, they'd taken insurance claims for ransom as well as hospital records. Unlike other "hacktivism" groups that insisted their cybercrimes were for good, the CryptTakers had suspected ties to terrorist groups.

"Preliminary background check shows your witness, a Bruce Walker, has no priors. Owner of the software company that provides banks with analysis software, divorced over a year ago, sole custody of his adopted daughter. No other family in town."

A mental image formed of a workaholic man in his early fifties with a teenage daughter. She knew the type. "So are we talking WITSEC or trial protection?"

"Assistant US Attorney thinks the moment the witnesses show up to testify, the guy will be ready to turn informant."

"So there must be a reason the hacker doesn't turn informant now."

"Exactly. The suspect implied he didn't think the witnesses would be able to make it to trial."

"A veiled threat, then. Matches the reputation of the CryptTakers."

"The other witness, Nancy King, commutes from Story City. We already have a team on the way. Your witness is located in Ames. I want you taking the lead on his detail."

Delaney nodded silently. She knew the Ames area best, likely better than the other marshals based out of Des Moines, but it still seemed like a big step to be appointed lead.

"Police are with your witness now. I'll tell them to expect you in an hour."

She hesitated to answer. "I'm actually in Ames now." She kept her gear packed and with her at all times. She never knew when a fugitive alert would come her way.

An uncomfortable silence followed. "That's good. Face those memories head-on."

Delaney cringed. Bradford didn't even have to be in the same room to see right through her. How was she supposed to impress a man who already knew all her faults?

"I'll send a car," he said. He rattled off the witness's address. "Since this is my stomping ground, feel free to consult me as well as the chief deputy with any questions. We're working tandem on this one. Two deputies will meet you there in an hour for transport to the safe house. I'll send the vetting information and case briefing as soon as I have them."

It would be the first time she'd ever served as lead on anything in the Marshals, which meant she couldn't let Marshal Bradford down. And being responsible for someone as important as a witness who could take down the CryptTakers caused a sudden craving for chocolate. Was there still a chocolate shop on Main Street? She shook off the thought and made a U-turn.

Bruce Walker lived in an older neighborhood near Squaw Creek, where the streets were lined with mature maple trees. She gawked at the house as she slowed to a stop. Unlike the typical farmhouse architecture on the street, his was a Tudor, a gorgeous piece of architecture the likes of which she'd only dreamed of ever owning. The steeply pitched gable roof, the curved wooden door, the decorative brick on the lower half and the chimney all hinted at simpler, more elegant times.

Given the age of the house, it wasn't a surprise the garage was unattached. A police cruiser was parked in the paved space between the garage and the house. A block away, an officer sat inside another cruiser strategically positioned at the curve, behind a twisted oak tree that jutted into the road.

Delaney braced herself. It'd been about three years since she'd been on the Ames police force, and during the last months of her service there, she'd been pregnant. Hopefully, the officers assigned to the protection detail were new recruits. She didn't want to rehash the past or go down memory lane with anyone. She stepped out of the rental car, held up her US Marshals badge in the direction of the cruiser and strode up the curved sidewalk to the front door.

A female officer she didn't recognize rounded the corner. "Ma'am, I'll need some identification."

Delaney displayed her badge and pulled out the rest of her ID. "I'll need the same from you."

The officer smiled and complied. "We heard you would arrive soon. I guess we'll let you take it from here. I'll be honest, though. I was looking forward to this assignment when I saw the cutie I'd be protecting."

Delaney felt her eyes widen at the unprofessional admission but said nothing. If this woman had been a fellow deputy, she might've pushed the issue. The officer waved her forward, and Delaney knocked on the door.

When it swung open, she fought to keep her face neutral. Bruce Walker looked nothing like the older man she'd imagined. At approximately six feet tall, a good five inches taller than she was, with wavy brown hair that barely curled over the top of his ears, light green eyes and olive skin, the man couldn't have been

more than thirty-five at the most. *He* was the owner of
the software company? That meant he was as smart
and capable as he was handsome. But while certainly
attractive, she wouldn't dare refer to him as a cutie.
His professional demeanor, broad shoulders and rugged
good looks demanded a much stronger descriptive word.

She held out a hand and Bruce's own hand enveloped
hers. "Deputy US Marshal Delaney Patton."

He held her fingers for a moment and tilted his head.
"Have we met?"

Her neck grew hot, and she dropped the stalled handshake before she could reflect on how his touch made
her stomach flip. "Not likely," she said. The one thing
she'd excelled at was remembering a face. The skill
helped when tracking down fugitives but wasn't going
to help tonight when she tried to fall asleep. Bruce's
green eyes were unforgettable.

"Sorry. You look familiar to me. I—"

"Daddy!" A high-pitched squeal and thundering footsteps came from the living room.

Bruce squatted down and caught the running toddler in his arms before standing up. "This is Winona."

"Winnie," the little girl announced, her forehead
creased in stern rebuke.

Bruce nodded. "But as you can tell, she likes Winnie
for short."

"Bye, cutie-pie." A voice rang out. Delaney turned
around to see the officer wave goodbye at the little girl.
So *that* was the cutie she'd meant. Delaney's cheeks
heated at her mistaken assumption.

"Winnie, honey, this is Mrs.—" Bruce's eyebrows
rose and he leaned forward toward her. "Sorry. Could
you repeat your last name?"

"It's Miss Patt—actually, Deputy Marshal Patton."

The little girl's face scrunched up in confusion. Delaney tried to smile but could feel her face fighting against it. Seeing the girl was like a punch to the stomach. The little one had to be the same age as her daughter would be.

She consoled herself with the fact that her newborn had had dark hair and the darkest blue eyes she'd ever seen, nothing like this child's light brown hair and sky blue eyes. Winnie wasn't her little girl, but her mind kept drifting, wondering if the couple who'd adopted her daughter lived somewhere in town—maybe next door, across the street, ten or fifteen minutes away. So close, yet with no way of reaching her, it might as well be another country. She steeled herself to focus on the present or she'd be useless.

"I guess the official name is pretty long," Delaney added. She'd never had to work with children before. "How about we keep it simple and you can call me Delaney?"

Winnie smiled shyly before she burrowed her face into her daddy's strong shoulder. "Come in," Bruce said. He turned and walked into the living room with a glance over his shoulder.

The living room took Delaney's breath away. Thick carpet soft enough that she was sure she could sleep on the floor without a pillow or blanket, a brown leather couch with thick teal blankets adorning each armrest, a wooden coffee table covered in both nonfiction tomes and picture books, and a fireplace at the opposite end of the room. If this was any indication of what the rest of the place was like, the house could serve as her dream vacation spot. Ceiling-high windows on either side of the mantel showcased a yard with a willow tree, an oak tree, sunflowers as tall as her witness, bird feeders and a wooden deck. A hummingbird zoomed up to one of the flowers, stole some nectar and darted away.

"I'm surprised they were able to send someone so soon," Bruce said, setting Winnie down. His phone vibrated. "Excuse me. My attorney said he'd get in touch and help walk me through this process. My company is in a very fragile state—"

So no one had let him know yet that he'd have to leave all his electronics behind. Did he even know they would need to leave, that they had a safe house waiting for them? She'd yet to see it, but knew without a doubt it would pale in comparison to his home.

Bruce held his phone up. From Delaney's vantage point she could see his entire screen had turned blue with white letters. Don't Open Your Mouth.

Delaney spun, assessing the windows and the exits. She locked the front door. "We can't afford to wait for the rest of the team." She leaned over furniture as she pulled down all the blinds over the front windows. The windows by the fireplace were without window coverings. "You have less than five minutes to grab a bag for you and your daughter. You're not safe here."

TWO

Bruce tried to keep his voice light, especially since Winnie stood next to him, but he struggled to keep his temper down. "I've spent the entire day away from my daughter. I've given the same statement over and over. They must've shuffled me around to a dozen people. The police have caught the shooter."

Bruce didn't even want to say Andy's name at the moment. The less he thought about what happened, the better he'd function. Max had been their security guard since Bruce opened the company. He felt a great sense of personal loss at the man's death, and it was all he could do to keep it together. "Can we take the panic down a notch?"

He paused as he thought about the warning on his phone. If Andy was in jail, then who'd sent the message to his phone? Maybe it was a relative or a girlfriend wanting to make sure her man didn't stay in prison. Though if that was the case, bringing in the Marshals to watch over them seemed a bit much. Delaney was acting as if he was in immediate, life-threatening danger. "Is there something I don't know?"

She flashed him a look of pity, but before he could

react, her pretty features hardened. "Normally, you would've been briefed by the Assistant US Attorney before I showed up, but we're on an accelerated schedule. Everyone is in catch-up mode. By Monday night, I'm sure all of that will have happened, but for now, you need to know my job is to keep you safe. There is a suspicion that the shooter has ties to a very dangerous group." She glanced down at the tactical watch on her wrist. "I'm giving you three minutes to grab what you need, or we leave with nothing and my team picks your clothes."

Bruce pulled his head back at the ultimatum. He could challenge her, but he could already see that she wouldn't back down. If the authorities thought Andy had dangerous allies, maybe he should get moving.

She stepped closer and lowered her voice. "Wouldn't you rather be safe than sorry?"

Her close proximity, gorgeous blue eyes and hushed voice soothed his nerves somehow. He took a step backward and smiled at Winnie. "Honey, go get your Lovey." While she ran for the blanket she insisted on sleeping with every night, he headed to his room and grabbed his biggest duffel bag. He darted from his dresser to the bathroom to Winnie's room.

The severity of the situation magnified with each item he threw in the bag. Maybe he should keep his mouth shut, pretend the murder and hacking attempt never happened and let the danger disappear. Though when the police had finally coaxed him and Nancy out of the server room, Max's lifeless form was still on the carpeted floor, blood pooled around his chest.

Bruce's limbs grew heavy, despite trying to move quickly. He couldn't allow a murderer to walk free, and he couldn't let Nancy take the burden of being the only witness. He had to testify.

He wanted to know which hacking group they suspected of being involved, but he wasn't sure it was a good idea to know. His stress levels were already through the roof.

Delaney stepped into the doorway of Winnie's room. "I've got officers waiting for us outside. It's time to go."

Winnie barreled into Delaney's right leg and squeezed. Bruce blinked in surprise. Winnie never ran to strangers, and she certainly didn't hug them.

Delaney flinched and stiffened. Winnie looked up and grinned. Delaney kept her head up and pursed her lips, as if she was about to be ill. Most women turned into putty around his adorable daughter, willing to do anything to earn more hugs and smiles from Winnie. Did the government assign him a marshal who hated kids?

Bruce dropped the duffel bag and scooped Winnie up. "You know, she's usually slow to warm to people. This is her way of letting you know she likes you."

Delaney frowned but didn't make eye contact. "Yes, thank you, uh…Winnie." She spun around and walked down the hallway to the front door while adjusting the hem at the back of her shirt. Bruce hadn't noticed the outline of a gun before. The reality that danger might be lurking in the trees around his home caused him to squeeze his daughter tighter.

He picked up the duffel bag and adjusted his hold in such a way that the bag mostly hid Winnie from sight. Delaney nodded in approval. "We'll have you and your daughter covered the whole way, but it's good to be cautious all the same." She jutted her chin toward

him. "I need you to leave all phones, laptops and tab-
lets here."

He'd anticipated as much after the phone message,
but he had clung to a thin hope that going entirely off
the grid wouldn't be necessary. He set all three of the
items she'd listed, along with chargers, on the couch,
but she didn't give him a chance to think further on
the matter.

"Someone will be by to pick up your phone. Hopefully we can trace that message." She waved a hand
toward the front door. "It's time." She stepped outside
and Bruce held Winnie tight as he followed.

Two officers flanked them, walking beside them
all the way to the back of a blue Ford Focus. A police
officer had apparently already retrieved the car seat
from Bruce's Ram truck in the garage and installed it
in the compact four-seater.

He ducked his head to squeeze inside and began
buckling in Winnie. The door closed behind him and
Delaney hopped into the driver's seat. "Ready?"

He snapped his own seat belt on. "Ready. I have to
say, I didn't realize the Marshals were so interested in
saving gas."

From the rearview mirror, he could see a lovely pink
shade cross her cheeks. "It's actually my rental car. I
just transferred back to the area. An official vehicle
will arrive for our use at the safe house." She pulled
away from the curve of the roundabout and drove out
of the neighborhood.

Winnie kicked her feet and released a high-pitched
whine. Bruce leaned over and examined the harnesses
to see if anything was pinching her. "What's wrong?"

She said nothing but pursed her little lips and

frowned at her shoes as she kicked rapidly again. Maybe her socks were bothering her. He had shoved her into the shoes pretty fast without making sure the seams were correct. He reached and tugged a bit on the cuffs. "Better?"

She stared at the shoes for another second before she nodded. He leaned against the seat. If only all of his problems were as easily solved as shoe discomfort. How was he going to manage staying in a safe house? Was he allowed to ask where the safe house was located or were questions like that frowned upon? Bruce wasn't accustomed to looking or feeling foolish or uninformed. He took great pride in researching every opportunity or purchase beforehand so that he always knew what he was getting into. It applied to his personal life, too, meaning his car was always stocked with extreme-weather gear, his house never lacked flashlights and extra batteries, and he never left the house with his daughter without bringing a bag full of snacks, toys and extra clothes.

Right now, though, all his emergency preparedness kits meant nothing. Instead, he was asked to rely on a woman he knew nothing about. "So you just moved back to the area?" he asked. "Maybe we did know each other at one point." He couldn't pinpoint it, but there was something about the way she moved or maybe her facial expressions…

"I used to work in the Ames Police Department, but it's been almost three years since I was on active duty. I suppose it's possible you saw me on patrol."

He leaned back in the vinyl seat, the top of his head almost brushing the fabric above him. He never re-called a police officer making enough of an impression on him to remember their face, especially three years later. She'd made a point of saying active duty—did that mean she spent some time off duty but still an officer? What reasons could there be aside from health issues or a suspension? "Are you new to the Marshals?" *Please say no.*

"No. I've been working in Coeur d'Alene, Idaho."

That didn't exactly make him feel better about her qualifications and experience. How many serious crimes could've happened in the Potato State? "Doesn't Idaho have more trees than people?"

She laughed. "Not sure about that. Definitely more *cattle* than people, but the same could be said for Iowa."

Fair point. "And pigs."

Delaney took a sharp turn around a corner and his daughter giggled. A lyrical laugh escaped Delaney before she pressed her lips together in a stern line. Bruce stared at the rearview mirror and tried to make sense of the woman. Did she like children or not? Perhaps it wasn't professional to appear happy when you were guarding people in danger.

She pulled up in front of an aging pink farmhouse. It was in the middle of nowhere—cut off from everything he was used to. Bruce purposefully lived his life focusing on the positive, but the bright side proved difficult to find at the moment. The loss of contact with his company and his employees hit him squarely in the chest. His throat tightened, but he forced himself to remain quiet until they stepped inside the dimly lit, musty-smelling house. He certainly hadn't expected luxury, but he'd hoped for a place comfortable enough that he could present it to his daughter as an adventure—a holiday. It would be downright impossible to imagine they were on vacation here. Delaney closed the door behind them and flicked on the light.

"How long is this supposed to last?" Almost all of his employees had families, and Bruce felt responsible for their financial stability. He already had to forgo the sales meeting Monday that could've provided millions in revenue. If the company failed in his absence, their livelihoods would be threatened. It wasn't as if he had a bunch of investors lined up to keep them afloat.

She bit her lip. "I can't really—"

"Please."

Her long brown ponytail swung to the left then the right as she looked around the room. A heavy sigh escaped her lips. "There are no guarantees, but there is the hope that this will only last until the trial."

"Which will be when?"

"I can't say. It usually takes two weeks to get the Marshals involved in a case. The fact that I'm here on the same day should tell you how important it is to the federal government to handle this matter swiftly."

Bruce's legs suddenly felt weak. He sat down on an ugly yellow-and-brown-striped love seat. Winnie climbed onto his lap. "Are you telling me we're being put into WITSEC?"

"No. At least, not right now. It's not off the table, though." A knock sounded on the door. She pulled out her weapon and peeked through an eyehole. "Friendly," she said softly as she reholstered the gun and opened the door.

The police officer on the porch reported a clear perimeter. "We got your stuff out of the trunk like you asked." He handed her a bright blue bag with the

Marshals logo on the side. She set it down next to the couch, unzipped it and retrieved a laptop.

"I thought electronics were frowned upon," Bruce commented.

"The Marshals make sure we use only the most secure devices."

So did he. It was tempting to argue with her, but he gave her the benefit of the doubt that she knew what she was talking about. Delaney sat down next to him on the couch, and Winnie reached her arms out for her.

He'd never seen his daughter act so forward, and he'd never seen a woman bolt so fast. Delaney popped up and moved to a wooden chair across the room. "I can probably type better over here."

Bruce wasn't so much offended as perplexed. Winnie didn't have a cold at the moment so it couldn't have been a germ-related phobia.

Delaney typed rapidly on her keyboard. "I'm afraid I need to get a few questions out of the way to provide the best protection possible. Do you have any loved ones in town?"

"Besides my daughter? No."

"What about your parents?"

He sighed. If only. "My mom remarried and retired in Arizona. My dad died when I was young."

Her gaze snapped up as if to comment but instead she returned to typing. "Your case file says you have a stepbrother."

Wow. They were going to hit on every sore point of his life in one swoop. This was going to be more fun than a visit to the doctor. "Trevor Schultz. He's also my former business partner. He asked me to buy him out six months ago. Last I heard he was catching rays in the Cayman Islands."

"I see you divorced over a year ago. Know the location of your ex-wife?"

"No."

Delaney stared at the screen for a bit before she looked back up. "Listen, I know this is hard. I really do. But I need to find out if there are any weaknesses someone might exploit to get to you."

If there was one thing Bruce had learned over the past couple of years, it was how to spot sincerity. He could see Delaney's genuineness. She hated asking the personal questions as much as he hated answering them.

He leaned over and pulled out Winnie's favorite pop-up book from the duffel bag, hoping it would keep his daughter distracted. "Shannon left over a year ago. She…" He let his voice trail off because he wasn't sure how to explain. Shannon had thought Bruce became boring after they got married. She'd wanted to live in Silicon Valley instead of the Silicon Prairie. She'd said she wasn't cut out to be a mother, but only brought that up *after* they had adopted a baby. He couldn't see a reason the Marshals would need to know all of those things. "Shannon left me for another man," he finally said. "I didn't ask who, and I honestly don't know where she landed."

Delaney's gaze flickered to Winnie and back.

"I have full custody." The fact was that Shannon didn't want anything to do with Winnie, something Bruce still couldn't understand.

Delaney twirled a strand of hair from her ponytail as she stared at the computer screen. It was a cute gesture that he doubted she did consciously. "How well did you know Andy Williamson before he was hired?" she asked.

"Not at all. In fact, Trevor hired him. He ran the daily operations of the company and had the final word in all marketing and HR matters. I took care of the product development."

"Did you socialize with Mr. Williamson after work hours—or speak to him about your own social behaviors? Any hobbies, activities or locations you frequent that he might have known about?"

"I don't do any socializing with my staff, and aside from the office, church and day care, no other recurrent locations." He used to have personal goals, aspirations...friends, even. There were more important things in life now.

Delaney blew out a breath as if gearing up for another onslaught of questions. "Dating?"

"No." It wasn't a ridiculous question. He'd thought about dating before, but how could he risk bringing another woman into Winnie's life after what had happened with Shannon? He didn't have the best track record at picking trustworthy people.

Her fingers flew over the keyboard. "What about the gym?"

He raised an eyebrow. "The gym?"

Delaney glanced at his arms before staring wide-eyed at her screen as if berating herself for looking at him. A fiery red began at her neck and worked its way upward. Bruce fought a grin, though he'd admit building muscle came relatively easy as long as he had time for strength work. "I have a jogging stroller. Otherwise, I work out with weights at home."

Delaney closed the laptop without comment and

avoided looking in his direction. "I think I'll check in with the team and see how close they are to arriving." She strode in and out of the bedrooms located on each side of the living room. "It looks like we need a portable crib, and I imagine you're getting hungry." She put her hands on her hips. "How about I have someone pick up some barbecue?"

Bruce didn't eat out often. He liked real food and found cooking relaxing. Besides, he hated to spend the money on restaurants if it was something he could cook, but the suggestion made his stomach growl. "If you know a place that's good."

She leveled him with a look that said "Trust me."

He answered the unspoken challenge. "I'm placing our safety in your hands. Obviously, I'm willing to trust you to pick the food."

Her bravado faded and her long eyelashes fluttered. She straightened as if bolstered with a new thought. "You won't regret it. I'll make sure of it."

Bruce felt certain neither one of them was thinking about the food anymore. She strode to the back door, one hand on her weapon and one hand on her phone.

He closed his eyes and nuzzled the top of Winnie's head as he prayed that, for once, he'd placed his trust in the right person.

Monday morning, Delaney pumped her arms in rhythm as she ran around the block. The weekend had been torture. She'd been assigned to protect the most handsome man and the cutest little girl on the planet. Every time Winnie smiled it felt like a vise around Delaney's heart, reminding her that she could've been a mother if only she'd gotten her life back together a little sooner. And Bruce…

Everyone liked Bruce. He stayed remarkably positive about their time cooped up in the house. He made comical faces to keep Winnie laughing and took turns playing two of the deputies in a game of Scrabble while the third was on patrol. He provided a list of groceries and made the most delicious stir-fry she'd ever tasted. In her line of work, often the witnesses had their own seedy, criminal pasts. While she appreciated their willingness to testify, it often stemmed from wanting to make a deal for themselves rather than from any genuine sense of public responsibility. But Bruce was a hardworking, upstanding…

She couldn't even let herself think about it or she'd start wishing for what she couldn't have. Deputy Marshal Francine Jackson and Deputy Marshal Jim Lewis were guarding Bruce and Winnie while she took an early morning run. It gave her a chance to clear her head and work out, but more important, to get a feel for the neighborhood and potential risk areas. Her phone buzzed and she slowed to a walk to answer. "Deputy Marshal Delaney Pat—"

"Delaney?" The male's voice shook on the line. "I, uh… I didn't expect to be talking to you."

"And this is?"

"Harvey Jeppsen."

An awkward silence followed. Harvey Jeppsen had been her lawyer for the private adoption. He'd been there with her in the hospital room when she'd signed away her legal rights to her baby. He'd listened to her sobs before and after. Why was he calling?

"I was told this is the number to contact my client,

Mr. Walker. Are you the marshal in charge?" His voice held a hint of disbelief.

Her shoulders dropped. "Yes. I'm afraid he's not able to talk right now. I can have him reach you in thirty minutes."

"No matter. I just received word he'll be at a pretrial interview later this afternoon with the US Attorney's Office. Please tell him I'll meet him there."

Delaney didn't confirm or deny, but she hung up only to get another call from the US Attorney's Office with the same information. It was last-minute, but in a case like this, that didn't surprise her. She jogged back to the safe house to start preparing for the trip. At least a brand-new black SUV with all the bells and whistles had arrived.

She imagined Bruce would be pleased with some forward motion on the case. It'd do him good to get out of the safe house for a bit. Maybe it would make him smile the way he had when... She cut the thought off abruptly. There she went again, thinking about his future facial expressions. The infatuation needed to be nipped in the bud. She lengthened her stride and reached the house in record time.

Thirty minutes later, she was showered, dressed and ready. "We probably should get going. I like to be extra early to allow time for contingencies."

Bruce frowned. He hadn't responded the way she'd expected. In fact, he seemed to be unhappy about going at all. "Any chance we can bring Winnie?"

"No." She didn't mean to snap. "Francine will stay here and take great care of her." Francine had fallen head over heels for Winnie. Unfortunately, Winnie acted as if she was set on making Delaney do the same. If she allowed herself to soften, she feared she'd be ruined when the case ended, devastated that she couldn't hold and snuggle her own little girl. "It will be a fast trip," she added.

A knock at the front door signaled it was time to go. The US Marshals had sent a fourth deputy to join in the transport. Bruce scratched his forehead. "Let me just put her down for her nap time."

Bruce picked up Winnie and kissed her little porcelain cheek. He started singing a song, tones so quiet and low that Delaney strained to hear it, but the concert wasn't for her. He disappeared into a side bedroom. A moment later he came out with a video baby monitor and handed it to Francine.

"Okay, she's singing to her stuffed animal, which means she should fall asleep soon. You have a way to reach me if I'm needed?"

Francine nodded. "Of course."

Delaney could see the uncertainty building in his eyes. "We have to go. Now," she said. Tag teaming with the deputy outside, she led Bruce to the door of the black SUV. They all wore plainclothes, which typically meant a polo shirt and pants, so as not to draw attention, but they didn't compare colors ahead of time. Unfortunately, the other marshals had all decided to go with navy blue, just as she had. If they needed somewhere to hide along the way, they could blend in at Best Buy.

A silver SUV was in front and a navy SUV was behind them. They would accompany her and Bruce to the federal building in Des Moines. She knew the route well enough to skip the GPS. "An hour's drive on I-35. I noticed they've widened the freeway since I've last been here. Should be smooth sailing."

She started the car and they drove in silence. A few minutes later, she merged onto the freeway. The other deputies spread out, so as not to be an obvious caravan, but they communicated their movements on the radio attached to the right of her steering wheel.

Much like a dentist was trained to watch for tense patients, she noticed Bruce's fingers gripping the sides of the leather seat and dug for something to say to distract him. "How long have you lived in Ames?" she asked. A small part of her wanted an excuse to ask how long Harvey Jeppsen had been his lawyer.

The brake lights flashed on the car in front of her. Delaney stepped on her own brakes and nothing happened. She shoved harder and the pedal went down to the floor, but their speed remained the same.

"What's happening?"

She couldn't answer because she wasn't sure herself, but the distance between the SUV and the car in front was rapidly decreasing. She slid into Neutral and pulled on the parking brake. The speed remained the same.

She glanced in the side mirror and maneuvered into the small spot between two cars. The radio crackled with questions, but she ignored them because the wagon in front of her wasn't going fast enough. She swerved onto the shoulder, almost clipping the car full of oblivious teenagers.

"One more inch and we would've hit. Sign says shoulder closed. Why are you doing this? Is there someone after us?" Bruce checked the side mirror.

She grabbed the radio with her right hand. "Brakes are out. Taking next exit." She dropped the radio as she used both hands to take the ramp, hoping the sharp curve to the right would slow them down or at least offer an empty pasture. "I can't talk now," she told Bruce.

The radio crackled. "Affirmative. We couldn't make that exit in time. Will take the next one and join you. No suspicious activity?"

"I think the brakes going out is suspicious enough," Bruce muttered. He leaned as far forward as he could and looked out the window. "There is a road to the left that's pretty unpopulated. Think you can make it?"

"We don't have much choice."

The grade sloped and the SUV's speed increased. She pressed the brake hard out of habit. Her head lurched forward and backward as the SUV abruptly slowed. She pressed the brake pedal again to make sure it wasn't a fluke. "The brakes are working again."

Bruce put his hand on the back of his neck. "Were you just not pressing hard enough?"

She bit back a retort and turned on her left signal. "It's safe to say that this SUV isn't as reliable as we'd like." They passed a gas station on the right. There was nothing but farmland on either side of the little-used highway. She tested the brakes again. Would the rest of the marshals think the whole event was the result of human error, as Bruce did? The vehicle jerked forward and a horrible grinding noise came from the hood. All the dials on the dashboard fell to zero as the motor went silent.

"The engine died?" Bruce shook his head. "Unbelievable. This isn't stick shift, is it? You didn't—" The rest of his words died on his lips.

Delaney followed his gaze, and her chest seized. A pickup truck full of masked men rounded the corner with guns pointed at their SUV.

"Get down!" Bruce gave her shoulder a push. While

the gesture was noble, she was supposed to be the one protecting him. She turned her head to see he'd followed his own advice as she readied her gun. Rapid pings hit the windshield, side doors and side mirrors.

"You okay?" Bruce asked. He remained hunched over, his forehead touching the glove compartment.

While the SUV was supposed to be bulletproof, she didn't want to take chances. "Yes. Stay down." The shots had stopped so she jumped out and took aim at the retreating vehicle, trying to read the license plate, but, of course, there was none. Not another vehicle could be seen for a mile in either direction. Where was her team? She kicked at a rock on the road and climbed back into the SUV.

While Bruce's face had lost its color, he didn't look injured. His hand shook ever so slightly as he pointed to the GPS. The blue screen had a message in the middle. Final Warning. Open your mouth and your family dies.

THREE

Bruce placed a hand on either side of his face. "It's been hacked."

She looked at him as if he'd lost his mind. "What are you talking about?"

He blinked and tried to slow down the torrent of emotions and thoughts so he could communicate rationally. "This vehicle has been hacked. The brakes, the engine dying, the message on the GPS... Those things can be controlled remotely if someone knows our location. They were playing with us. My daughter—" He pulled in a shaky breath. They'd only been gone from the safe house for five minutes. If someone had been tracking them in the vehicle, then it was likely the hacker knew their point of origin.

Her eyes widened. "The safe house. You're saying the attackers know where it is." She picked up the handset. "We've been compromised. I need a new vehicle, stat. Where are you guys?"

The speakers crackled in response. "You're not going to believe it. Our engines died the moment we got off the highway."

"Both of them?" Delaney took a deep breath while

she checked all three mirrors. Bruce followed her gaze. So far the gunmen hadn't returned. "They set us up." Delaney pulled out her cell phone and dialed the police for backup. After the call was completed, she sat back, shaking her head. "I don't understand how this could be happening."

"Newer cars have a few different ways hackers can access control. If this one has a tire sensor, that's the simplest way to hack into the brakes and disable the engine." He waved toward the hood of the car. Talking about practical matters wasn't helping his heart rate. If he thought he could get back faster on his own, he'd try to run back to Winnie on foot. "I need to know Winnie is okay. I need to know now."

"There are two deputy marshals watching over her. I'm sure Winnie is safer than we are at the moment. It's safer if we don't make direct contact." She clicked the radio. "I need a status report from Deputy Marshal Jackson. Use back channels."

They sat in tense silence for the longest thirty seconds of his life before the radio crackled. "No response as of yet," the deputies from the other SUV answered. "Backup units on the way from Des Moines."

Bruce tightened his fists. "From Des Moines?" He couldn't wait an hour to find out if his daughter was safe or in the hands of dangerous criminals.

"Bruce, you've been great so far. Look at me."

Bruce swiveled and stared into Delaney's eyes, searching for answers.

She touched his arm. "We aren't waiting around. The police will be here in one minute. Sometimes back channels take longer to get an answer. We can't jump to conclusions."

Bruce exhaled, but his insides wouldn't stop vibrating. Winnie was his all, his everything. She had stolen his heart from the moment he held her tiny form in his arms.

As promised, a police cruiser pulled up, but Delaney wouldn't let him step out of the SUV yet. She kept her hand on her weapon as she approached the vehicle, likely checking the officer's identification. Every moment of procedural caution made him want to jump out of his skin, but if he complained or fought it, he would just cause more delay. *Lord, please, just get me to Winnie. Keep her safe.*

He opened his eyes as Delaney opened the door. "I'm afraid the back seat of a police car isn't very comfortable."

He grunted and walked behind her to the unit. He'd walk on glass if it'd get him to his daughter faster. Bruce slipped into the back seat. Delaney slammed the door and joined the cop in the front.

"No sirens, but get to this address as fast as possible," Delaney said.

The officer didn't hesitate to punch the gas. Bruce slid across the plastic bucket seats and grasped the seat belt with one hand during the U-turn. At least Delaney was taking the threat seriously. At this rate, they really would be back to the safe house quickly.

"Uh, how are you doing?" the policeman asked Delaney. "We've missed you on the force."

Even from the back seat, the look Delaney shot the other officer seemed made of ice. "I'm fine."

"We miss Raymond, too, you know," the officer said.

She nodded but didn't reply. Bruce wondered if the words that hinted at tragedy explained her aloof demeanor toward him and Winnie. Not that it really mattered. He didn't need Delaney to care about him and his daughter—he just needed her to protect them, as she'd said she would. But was that a promise she'd keep? Words didn't mean much compared to action.

His wife had promised so much, but she still left him and Winnie without a second glance. His stepbrother had written his company's mission statement and promised to be his partner, but he'd quit and run to the Cayman Islands six months ago. No, promises really didn't mean much.

Delaney turned in her seat to face him, an impressive feat given the high-speed turns. "The Marshals are alerting the Assistant US Attorney to what's happened. The interview will be rescheduled."

"I can't even think of testifying at the moment."

"So don't think about it. For now."

The radio crackled but Bruce couldn't make out what was said.

"Did something happen?"

"Not necessarily. Deputy Marshal Jackson still hasn't checked in, so we're going to proceed with caution." Delaney pointed to the left, and the cruiser stopped at the sun-bleached pink house. The last two days had felt like a living nightmare. He'd worked so hard to maintain a positive attitude and believe that everything would work out, only to walk straight into a trap.

"Stay here," Delaney hollered. She jumped out of the vehicle at the same time as the officer.

"That's not happening." Bruce reached for the car handle but found there was none. He pounded the seat in frustration. Another police vehicle pulled up at the opposite street corner, and two more cops rushed toward the house.

Delaney held her weapon up and gestured at the other officers to go around the building. A male voice shouted, "Officer down," and Bruce groaned. Someone had definitely found the safe house. *Please, let Winnie be okay.* He searched desperately for another way out of the police vehicle, but there was nothing to do but watch.

Delaney squatted low to the ground and entered the house. Bruce strained his eyes, hoping he could somehow see past the house's grimy windows and blinds. Sirens sounded in the distance. He couldn't look away, couldn't let himself blink. He should be inside there, protecting his daughter.

An officer sauntered toward the cruiser that was holding him prisoner. Bruce clenched his jaw, wanting to yell at him to speed up. The officer reached his hand out and the door trapping him in the back seat finally swung open.

"The Deputy Marsh—"

Bruce vaulted out of the car into a sprint, past the officer. He vaguely heard the man shout but didn't care what was being said. Right now, the only thing that mattered was Winnie. An ambulance siren's wail grew closer.

He barreled into the house, squinting in the dim light. Another deputy, Francine, was on the ground, limp but conscious. A cop held her wrist while looking at his watch to count her pulse.

Delaney stepped out of a bedroom. Her arms cradled Winnie, her head bent over his daughter, as if in a cuddle. Bruce's insides fought between icy cold and raging heat at the sight.

She glided forward, her steps soft and rhythmic, across the room, whispering, "It's okay, sweetheart." One of Winnie's arms wrapped around the back of Delaney's neck while the other clung tightly to Lovey. "Winnie, your daddy is here."

Winnie lifted her head and twisted to look. She blinked twice and smiled at Bruce, then rested her head back on Delaney's chest.

"She was still sleeping," Delaney whispered. "Had no idea anything happened." Her eyes glistened with a layer of unshed tears and once again Bruce didn't know what to think or feel about this mysterious woman.

He reached for Winnie. His daughter, almost reluctantly, let go of Delaney and curled up against his chest. "Honey, are you okay?"

She nodded and rubbed the remaining aftereffects of sleep away.

Delaney stepped closer. "Someone got the jump on them. Knocked out the marshals but didn't touch Winnie."

Bruce crumpled onto the couch. He hung his head over Winnie's shoulder and, despite the determination to stay calm, his chest shook and his breath caught. He could've lost her. He so easily could've lost her.

Winnie tilted her chin and Bruce stared into her blue eyes and reined in control. Was there a way he could give up and keep her safe? If he didn't testify, would the threat disappear?

"I appreciate that you stayed calm today," Delaney said.

He didn't look up. He couldn't yet. "If you lock me in the back of a car again…" He let his voice trail off, unwilling to voice exactly what he was thinking in front of his daughter, but hoping his tone conveyed what he meant. He wouldn't let her keep him away from Winnie again.

But even by his side, could he keep his little girl safe? Could he ever take Winnie with him on a jog and count dogs in the neighborhood without flinching at every car that rounded the corner? Would they be able to return home and step out onto the deck to watch fireflies without him shining a spotlight on every tree that surrounded the property first?

The image of the men with guns shooting bullets into the SUV played on a loop. His blood pounded hot and fast through his veins. Giving in would only provide the illusion of safety. They would still be out there, watching. They could treat him, his daughter and anyone else like puppets whenever they wanted. Good men like Max would still die at their hands.

The rage continued to build behind his eyes. He would do whatever it took to put a stop to them. He slowly met Delaney's gaze. "How do we end this?"

Delaney's mouth went dry at his question. Winnie clutched her Lovey in one hand while her other hand twirled a lock of hair. Delaney did that whenever she was stressed or bored, too. Was that common in toddlers? Movement to the right caught her attention.

Two paramedics filled the doorway. The taller one nodded at Delaney. "We've got one of the deputies ready for transport."

She supplied his name. "Deputy Jim Lewis."

The medic pointed to Francine. "We can take you on that ambulance, too, ma'am. In the meantime, anyone else we need to look at?"

Francine flicked her wrist. "I don't need it. I'm going to be fine."

"Wait," Delaney said. "You might not need an ambulance, but we do." She held up a hand to stop the concerned paramedics. "I don't mean we're injured. For logistic reasons, I need you to hang back for a second."

Delaney pointed at Bruce. "Right now the main priority is to get you somewhere safe without being tracked. You said hackers can follow our vehicles if they know the point of origin, so we need to make sure they think we're still here. At least for a little while." She felt a pressure on her chest and realized she'd kept a hand over her heart, in the place where Winnie had rested her head moments ago.

"What do you have in mind?" Francine asked. She accepted an ice pack from the paramedic and rested it on the back of her head.

"Bruce and Winnie will take your place on the stretcher, covered up." She squatted slightly to meet the toddler's eyes. "Can you be real still next to your daddy and pretend you're sleeping?"

Winnie pulled her left shoulder up until it met her ear in a cute shrug. "No." She smiled, but her eyes made it clear she had no intention of cooperating.

Well. There went that idea, replaced with a sizable dose of reality. Delaney knew nothing about children.

Bruce patted Winnie's knee. "You don't have to take a nap again," he said. "How about we play hide-and-seek together and wait for Delaney to find us? Those men are going to sneak us out, like a fun ride."

Winnie's eyes widened and she bounced up and down. "Okay."

The side of Bruce's mouth curved. "It's all in the delivery."

Francine laughed, a welcome distraction and a comfort. She probably wouldn't have laughed if she was seriously injured, but Delaney would make sure she was examined anyway.

"Francine, I need you to stay back here for a good twenty minutes. When it's time to leave, tuck your hair up into a ball cap and wear Bruce's suit jacket." Delaney turned to ask the man in question. "Do you mind?"

"It'll be too big on her, but no, I don't mind."

Francine was a tall woman, equal to Bruce's height, but she had a slender build. "I know. It won't be enough to fool anyone at close examination, but if anyone's watching from a distance, it should at least give them pause." She pointed at the police officer waiting next to her. "It would help the Marshals a great deal if you'd wait here a bit, then take Francine to the station. I'll have another deputy meet her there and take her to the hospital to be examined."

Francine rolled her eyes. "I told you I'm fine—"

"I need you back on the team as soon as possible," Delaney answered. According to Marshal Bradford, Francine was the only deputy who had experience with children. "That means you need to get cleared for duty."

"I'd like to apologize in advance." Bruce stood up, Winnie in his arms, to head over to the stretcher. "I'm not a lightweight man."

The paramedic to the left laughed. "Don't worry. The stretcher pops up and has wheels. Besides, we've carried heavier. You ready for your ride, sweetie?"

Delaney stilled, unable to look away. Was this the right

decision? The paramedics joked around with Winnie as Bruce got situated first on the gurney.

She was up against clever hunters. As soon as word got out that Bruce wasn't backing out of testifying, the hacking group would be after them again. What would Kurt do? The question popped into her mind easily, as it always did whenever she faced a crisis in her work. Her previous boss and mentor from Coeur d'Alene, Kurt had taught her more than her time in both the police academy and marshal training. He'd showed her when it served best to think outside of the box, to harness empathy and to understand what the enemy would do next to get a jump on them. He also sought God's wisdom for the big decisions.

Her throat hurt from the stress. *I don't have time to wait to hear from You, Lord. I'm asking for Your wisdom and if I'm going the wrong way I need a giant "no" from You right about now.*

"Let's hide, Daddy." Winnie turned to Delaney and smiled. "You gotta find us." She grabbed the edge of the thin white blanket and pulled it over herself as she curled up in the crook of Bruce's arm.

The paramedics placed a mammoth-sized towel on Bruce's forehead, effectively covering up his face and hair. It didn't make him look like Francine, but it might do the trick. Delaney grabbed her US Marshals jacket and placed it on top of him. If anyone was watching, hopefully it would seem another marshal was heading for the ambulance after the attack.

"Okay, stay real quiet. We're going on a ride and don't want Delaney to find us yet," Bruce said.

"I think that's our cue." The paramedic at the helm kicked off the brakes. Delaney kept her head up as she jogged beside them. No cars were in sight and nobody hid in any of the trees. The houses were spread out and all had curtains or blinds down to help keep out the high-noon heat. But who knew what resources a group of hackers had to watch wherever they wanted? There could be eyes on them right now. The thought sent a shiver up her spine.

A toddler-shaped lump on Bruce's side wiggled and giggled. Thankfully they'd reached the back of the ambulance. The paramedics shoved the gurney up the silver ramp into the ambulance.

Deputy Jim Lewis had a seat on a gray bench with an ice pack on the back of his head. "I don't know how they got a jump on me." His eyes implored her to understand. "I'll be more cautious now, you can count on that. You're the lead. You can waive procedure and tell me I don't have to get checked for a knock on the head so I can get back to work."

"Not a chance." She took a seat beside him as the doors closed behind them. "You're staying right here in this ambulance, because I'm going to need you in a moment."

One paramedic sat on the opposite side of the stretcher as the ambulance began to move. Winnie flung down the sheet and popped upright. "Find me." As fast as she'd appeared, she vanished with giggles. "Daddy, you hide, too."

"It's definitely time for you to find us." Bruce's muffled voice came from underneath the sheet that now covered his face.

Delaney's chest seized, as if a hard, protective layer around her heart was being ripped apart, one tiny square at a time. The paramedic and Jim watched her with anticipation. She leaned forward and pulled back the blanket to find Winnie's wide eyes. "Found you," she said softly.

Winnie twisted so her face smashed against Bruce's side, but the little girl's laughter would not be contained and proved contagious to the other occupants of the ambulance.

The paramedic beamed and leaned back into his seat. "I tell you what, young lady. We don't usually have a lot of laughter in the back of this vehicle. Would make my job a lot easier if we did." He leveled a pointed look at Delaney. "We're almost to the hospital if you need to arrange a ride."

"Of course." She pulled out her phone. "Jim, I need you to switch places with Bruce."

Jim began to object.

"You're taking his place as an added precaution, so we can slip away unnoticed. Bruce, put on the marshal's hat."

Bruce sat up and tried to hand Winnie to her. She froze until the little girl reached out her arms. Delaney's back tensed but she reached forward and took Winnie. It wasn't a big deal to hold the little girl so the men could switch positions without kicking someone in the head. Logically, she knew that.

It felt dangerous, though. It was becoming harder and harder not to think about her own daughter out there somewhere. Delaney had a little over fifteen years left before she could ask for the sealed adoption records to be opened.

"Let's play hide again," Winnie said.

"Maybe after we're in the hotel, okay?" A hotel wasn't ideal, as it required a lot more manpower to adequately protect a witness, but she didn't have another safe house arranged in town. The less they had to travel, the better.

She dialed the chief deputy's number and hoped the second team on the way had an extra vehicle for her. Every moment spent in the hospital—the very place where she'd delivered her daughter—would be torture. Even thinking about it, she could smell the phantom aromas of antiseptics and disinfectants. Her scars remembered the tenderness and pain after the emergency surgery. Winnie snuggled closer, and the smell of baby shampoo in her hair shifted Delaney's focus.

The chief deputy answered, and she wasted no time outlining her plan to keep Bruce and Winnie safe. She held her head high as she spoke and hoped no one could hear the fear and doubt lacing every word.

FOUR

Bruce strode from one end of the hotel room to the other. He could cross the entire room in five and a half steps. If they allowed him to open the curtains to watch strangers walk past, he'd have something in common with zoo animals. Though the animals likely ate healthier food than the fast food he'd been served.

The connecting door opened and Delaney stepped inside, holding up his black duffel bag. He placed a finger over his mouth. Delaney's gaze moved to the center of the bed where Winnie had, mercifully, fallen asleep for the night.

"Officers brought your stuff over."

He accepted the duffel gratefully. "She'll be glad to have her things." While the front desk had provided a toothbrush, Winnie had thrown a royal fit that she didn't have her normal toiletries for her bedtime routine. They'd left in such a hurry that she didn't even have her shoes to wear. And, of course, he felt like a horrible dad for not having realized it until after they stepped out of the ambulance.

She was a lightweight thing until he had to hold her when she desperately wanted down. The nurses pro-

vided bootees so Winnie could "skate" down the hallway while he held her hand. It had been almost a full
hour before they were escorted via an unmarked van
to the hotel's back entrance.

If they'd removed the letterhead and pens from the
room, he wouldn't even have known which inn they'd
crashed at for the night. He genuinely hoped it would only
be for one night. Reality, combined with the greasy pizza
he'd had for dinner, used his stomach as a punching bag.

Delaney regarded him, a smile playing on her lips.
"Aside from the threat, most people would be happy to
spend a day at a hotel."

"Really? Enlighten me."

"Well, they kick back on the pillow top, eat junk
food, enjoy a good TV binge session and relax."

He found it hard to believe that the deputy was better than he was at relaxing. "I don't watch anything on
TV unless you count half watching various preschool
programs."

Her mouth stretched wide to reveal a dazzling smile
that lit up her entire face. "If you had said Pixar mov-
ies, I would've let it slide, but I'm afraid preschool programming doesn't count."

He couldn't help but match her grin. "Hey, some
of those have pretty good plots. What do you watch?"

She grew quiet. "Well, I haven't had a chance lately,
but I'm sure there are some good shows out there."

He'd called it. She was like him—a workaholic.
Though he hadn't always been that way. There was a
time, not too long ago, when he'd enjoyed lounging.
He used to place value on daydreams, personal goals,
aspirations and even wish lists. Now his life revolved

around work and his responsibilities to Winnie. Not that those things didn't bring him joy, but—

"Are you going to wake her to put on her pajamas?" Delaney continued to stare at Winnie, tilting her head in curiosity. Her voice had a soft, soothing timbre to it.

"No. Though I'll set them out in case she wakes in the middle of the night demanding them." He kneaded the stiff muscles on the side of his neck. Impending tension knots and pain could be avoided with a good run, but even if they let him use the hotel gym, he wouldn't leave Winnie in the room. "By the way, I'm not going anywhere without her from now on. The Marshals can stay with her at the courthouse as easily as they could at some safe house."

Her smile disappeared. "I really don't think it's a good idea."

"Why not?"

"For one, I'm the one in charge of staying with you, and I don't do kids." She pulled her shoulders back and the hardness returned, shrouding her features.

"Sure you do. Winnie likes you."

Her left eyebrow lifted, but she didn't engage. "If we can figure out how they found us in the first place and protect against it happening in the future, you'll have no reason to worry anymore. The only electronic device we found in the safe house was the video baby monitor that you brought." Delaney pulled out a chair and sat at the table.

"You're not implying the hackers used the monitor to—"

"I'm only presenting the facts."

He didn't like that insinuation. "That's a one-to-one

communication device. It can't be hacked to find our location."

"Our tech guy agrees with you on that point. But if they had tracked our location already, they could've hacked the monitor to eavesdrop, watch to see when we left and get a jump on the two marshals we had stationed with Winnie." Her eyes widened. "Looks like someone is up."

Winnie bounced on the giant bed behind Bruce and flopped down spread-eagled on the mattress. Then she jumped up to do it all over again. Bruce groaned. Now that she was this hyped-up, it would take hours to get her back to sleep again. Her giggles made it hard to mind too much, though. His little girl didn't have a care in the world, the way it should be. He, however, wouldn't be able to rest until he knew how the criminal organization tracked them down in the first place.

Delaney bit her lip and jotted something down on the hotel notepad. "Has Harvey Jeppsen been your personal lawyer for quite some time?"

Bruce tried to see what she'd written, but she was still writing. "He's the company lawyer," he answered. "I suppose we've been connected for the past five years, but it's not really common knowledge."

Her face fell, almost as if she was disappointed. "So, he hasn't been your personal lawyer up until now?" she asked.

"No, not really. He's been an advisor occasionally but he's never billed me for questions I've asked him on personal matters." The only things he'd needed a lawyer for had been Winnie's adoption and his divorce. Harvey had referred him to a different lawyer for the adoption, and the divorce had been handled without lawyers since

Shannon didn't ask for anything. She'd just wanted out of the marriage…and motherhood. "Why is it important? Are you suggesting the hackers bugged Harvey's phone and traced outgoing calls?"

"I don't know. I'm examining all the possibilities."

If his lawyer proved to be the weak link in security, he could remedy that. "I'm happy to tell Harvey to stay out of this. I don't even need a lawyer. It only seemed wise to have one in the first place because the murder and malware attempt happened on my company's property and—"

"Bruce," she said softly. "It's not necessary to waive any rights. We've added more safeguards. I've already been given a new phone and a new number. Your lawyer has agreed to being paged at the last minute. The Marshals will transport him to your trial interview. Making it last-minute will hopefully decrease the risk of any further attempts."

"What about Nancy?" He berated himself for not having thought of her sooner.

"Nancy," Winnie shouted, looking around the room.

"No, honey, she's not here," Delaney said. She leaned back in her chair and looked surprised at herself. Apparently, the term of endearment had just slipped out. Bruce couldn't help the smile on his face either. She might try to act hard and professional, but no one could resist liking his sweet Winnie. Not even someone who feigned disliking kids.

Her side glance had to have seen his smile, but she ignored it. "Mrs. King is safe."

"Has she had—" he searched for a word that wouldn't scare his daughter "—*incidents* like ours?"

"Her pretrial was scheduled after ours so we don't

know if her location had been compromised. She's been moved to another safe house as a precaution, but other than that, it's been quiet."

A small knock at the hotel door sounded. Delaney stood in one smooth motion, her hand at the small of her back. "No reason for concern," she said, but she kept her eyes on the door. "Please make sure Winnie doesn't follow me, though."

Delaney stepped to the door's peephole and found an officer she knew from her days on the force waiting in the hallway. She exhaled and turned back to Bruce. "Excuse me a moment."

Delaney stepped into the hallway and closed the door behind her.

"It really is you," the police officer said. "Been a long time. Good to see you're doing well, kiddo."

Delaney bit back a retort and focused on trying to remember his name. "Fred," she said. "Good to see you, too." The Ames Police Department had agreed to help the Marshals by loaning their SWAT team until more deputies could be sent to the area.

"The feds want a word with you," he said. "We took their badge numbers and ran their identifications through the computer. They're really FBI. It all checked out." He gestured at two men in suits who were walking down the hallway in her direction.

"You're sure their IDs are legit?"

"Even their photos."

But the FBI shouldn't be anywhere near her witness while he was in protective custody. Knowledge of his location was meant to be as limited as possible. She found it hard to believe that the Marshals and US Attorney's

Office would blatantly disregard protocol without first informing her. "How about you stay here while I chat with them?" She gave the approaching agents a smile and nod as they quickly closed the distance. "Deputy Marshal Patton. How can I help you?" She didn't offer a handshake but kept her hands on her hips, so she could grab her weapon fast, if needed.

The first suit gestured at the door behind her. "That Mr. Walker's room?"

"No, it's mine," she answered and hoped Fred didn't reveal her falsehood. The rooms to either side of Bruce and Winnie were reserved for the Marshals. At night, Delaney would take the room directly across the hall. "Mind telling me how you two came to find us here?"

"Word from on high," the agent on the right answered. "We need to talk to Mr. Walker immediately. We're investigating a related crime."

Witnesses were sometimes interviewed by different departments for related crimes, but any FBI agent worth their salt would've known to fill out such a request with the US Attorney's Office first.

So either both of the agents in front of her were poorly trained newbies, or they weren't agents at all. "Word from on high" was about as vague an answer as she'd ever heard.

She smiled sweetly. "What case are you working on?" she asked.

The first agent seemed surprised by her friendliness before exchanging a glance with his partner. She used the opportunity to calculate how many weapons they each carried. The guy on the left side had at least two guns, judging by his gait when he'd walked down the hallway, but the guy on her right only had one that she noticed.

Her first order of business would be to lead them away from Bruce's room. All other hotel occupants had been moved to a different floor, and thankfully, since there were no sports events happening throughout the weekend to book up the rooms, they had been able to clear the entire east wing on the main floor. If she managed to escort the agents farther down the hallway, the SWAT team members would be more readily available to assist.

The second man narrowed his gaze on Delaney. "It's confidential. Can we speak to Mr. Walker now?"

"Of course," she said, practically cooing. "You'll just need to check your weapons in with the officer here, and I'll take you right to him." She gestured at Fred, whose stern frown conveyed his confusion, but he made the slightest adjustment of hand placement, which she knew from experience meant his index finger had unlocked his holster.

She turned back to the agents and gave them a nonchalant wave. "But I'm sure I didn't need to tell you that. Procedure, of course."

The first "agent" pulled out his gun so fast Delaney only managed to grab the handle of hers in the holster. His partner had a gun pointed at her, as well. Delaney prayed that Fred had managed to draw his own gun or she was out of options.

Bruce's hands pressed against the door on either side of the peephole. Despite the warped fish-eye view, he could see two guns were pointed at Delaney. He shoved himself backward, ran to the unlocked connecting door

and barged in without knocking. A new deputy marshal—
he'd yet to learn the name—sat at a round table, cleaning
weapons. The man's hands froze at the sight of Bruce,
but he didn't say anything.

"Two men have guns aimed at Delaney and another
police officer in the hallway, right in front of my door."

The marshal muttered some words that Bruce hoped
his daughter hadn't heard, but the deputy's weapons
were loaded and ready in three seconds flat.

"You probably don't want to startle them," Bruce
added, one foot already back inside of his room.

"Stay in there and let me do my job." The man crept
toward his own front door. Bruce darted to pick Winnie
up off the bed. Giggles from their room would certainly
raise the suspicions of the men with guns. "Honey, let's
play hide-and-seek." He picked her up and whispered,
"I'm going to hide you and then count to ten and find
you. Be really quiet, okay?"

Her smile lit up her entire face as she nodded rapidly.
Bruce had heard tales of the terrible twos, but so far
he loved that she could be redirected to something else
in a heartbeat. She also didn't care to understand the
rules of hide-and-seek. He set her down on the floor of
the closet. "Okay, you have to be super quiet and stay
there. I'll come find you soon."

Thankfully, his statement made perfect sense to
Winnie. She pressed her tiny hands over her face, light
laughter seeping out.

Bruce searched the room for something, anything,
to help Delaney. His eyes rested on a solitary piece
of stationery next to the television set. Hotels often
slipped bills underneath the doors in the morning. If
something could be slipped under the doors, surely it

could be slipped back out into the hall. He picked up the blank piece of paper and checked on the hallway situation through the peephole. Delaney's voice carried through the door as she shouted at the men. "I suggest you put down your weapons and tell me what you're really doing here."

His instinct was to fling the door open and slam his fists against the chins of the men who threatened her. He barely contained the impulse.

The gunman closest to the door said, "Not happening."

If he could distract the gunmen for just a second, maybe the other deputy could help...

He leaned over and shoved the piece of paper under the door and out into the hallway.

Bruce hopped back up to peek out the door. The gunman closest to the door glanced down to see the paper. Delaney took a step closer to him. What was she thinking? Would Bruce's attempt at creating a distraction get her hurt? He wasn't sure he could watch Delaney get killed. His hand reached for the hotel door handle.

FIVE

Delaney didn't care what the paper was that she'd stepped on. It couldn't have come at a better time. Deputy Marshal Sanders had slipped out of the hotel room behind the fake agents with his gun firmly trained on the agent to her left, who held Fred at gunpoint. Deputy Sanders and Fred could team up and take that agent while she handled the one right in front of her.

She locked eyes with the gunman, whose expression showed that he had realized his mistake in looking down at the paper. He snarled and lifted his gun to aim, but she slapped both of her hands around his extended arm.

She flipped the gun out of his hand and into hers, a half-second maneuver she'd practiced hundreds, if not thousands, of times. She slammed the butt of the gun into the man's stomach, grabbed his neck with her other hand and yanked it down as she pulled her knee up until it connected with his nose. He bellowed and grabbed his face.

She took a step back to point the gun at him but another body plowed into her from the side. Her shoulder and head slammed into Bruce's hotel door. The deafening ring of two gunshots served to further disorient her.

"Stop!" Deputy Sanders aimed his weapon at something beyond her scope of vision and took a shot. Where were the gunmen?

Delaney twisted against the weight pressing against her legs. Fred had collapsed against her. He groaned and held a hand over his heart. She dropped to her knee, using her body as a fulcrum to press him upright so she could get around him. "Are you hurt?"

Despite his sweat-covered face, he shook his head. "Vest," Fred whispered.

The door that held their weight gave way and she fell backward into strong arms. Bruce's face appeared over hers as he dragged her into the safety of the hotel room. Bruce would've made a wonderful fireman, judging by the ease with which he carried her. Having someone watch out for her well-being unleashed a longing for companionship she didn't know she had, but she couldn't reflect on it.

"What are you doing?" She scrambled to her feet and shut the door behind her. "Someone could've seen you."

Bruce gestured toward the hallway. "I heard gunshots and you fell against the door. I thought you were hit."

"Daddy, find me," Winnie's voice, though muffled, called out. Just hearing the child's voice drove the truth of the situation home.

He was her protectee. A piece of evidence was to be in a vault, kept safe and free from any compromising influence so as not to be altered. She was to see to her witness in the same manner. "Take Winnie into the other room. Lock it up tight. Don't open the door for anyone."

He nodded. As soon as Bruce and Winnie disappeared through the connecting door and the bolt clicked, she darted back into the hallway. On the ground to her right, the gunman that had squared off with Fred and Sanders was slumped on the floor at an odd angle. She scanned past the blood on his shirt to find his wide-open eyes devoid of life.

Fred stood up but still had a hand to his chest.

She tried to make sense of the scene in front of her. "The fake agent tried to shoot me and you jumped in front of the bullet while Sanders took him down. You saved my life."

Fred nodded but said nothing. The pounding in her head grew louder. Shouts from other officers down the hallway fought for her attention. Another gunshot in the distance sounded.

The gun she'd removed from the first assailant had slipped from her fingers when Fred had barreled into her, and she didn't take time to look for it. She twisted her torso and retrieved her own weapon. Were more gunmen coming?

Deputy Sanders rounded the corner at the end of the hallway with his hands up. "There was another exit just past the vending machines. He got away."

"You're telling me the man that I disarmed got away? How is that possible?" Frustration mounted. "I *had* him."

"You *had* him while his partner was about to blow you away," Sanders snapped. "I shot the assailant while the officer took a bullet for you, and the second gunman slipped past me."

Delaney hung her head. Two fellow law enforcement officials had risked their lives to save hers. She didn't need to express her aggravation that one of the men got away. They had to be feeling it, as well.

"He won't get far, though," Sanders added. "I know I hit him as he ran. We'll have all hospitals in a two-hundred-mile radius on standby."

The moment of adrenaline started to fade as fast as it had started. "Thank you," she said to Sanders. "Thanks to both of you," she added to Fred.

"You'd have done the same for us." Fred still held a hand over his vest.

"They've got an ambulance coming to check on you," Sanders said to Fred.

Delaney put her hands over her face for a second. Unbelievable. Her first case acting as lead and not only did fake agents get through a police barricade, one got away. She couldn't even use the one they did have as a witness, seeing as how he was dead and all.

She probably shouldn't open with that when she called in to headquarters.

A more terrifying thought emerged. If the hackers could get into law enforcement databases and forge federal agent identifications, she wouldn't be able to trust anyone she didn't already know.

The alternate bursts of static and voices from Fred's police radio served as an incessant reminder that the next few hours would be steeped in paperwork and phone calls. At least the ability to delegate was one benefit of serving as lead deputy. "Sanders, please serve as liaison with the police. I need to check on our witness."

Delaney removed the key card from her pocket and prayed Winnie wouldn't be traumatized by what had just occurred. She pressed the handle until the door reached the limit of the safety latch. "Bruce, it's me."

He leaned out of the bathroom door until he saw her face, then stepped out, holding a rifle at the side of his right leg.

She jolted at the sight and pointed at the weapon. "Where'd you get that?"

"The deputy left it on his table." He closed the door to remove the latch before he reopened it to face her. "I've never used one, but I figured a stranger wouldn't know that." He gingerly placed the rifle on the top shelf of the closet as she closed the door behind her.

The events replayed in her mind. Her heart pumped faster. She stepped closer to him. "So you were watching through the door that whole time?"

His eyes widened and he pulled his head back. "Not the whole time. The rest was spent hiding, 'finding' and rehiding Winnie so she would stay quiet." He folded his arms and gave her an appreciative nod. "Though I would love to learn how you flipped that gun out of the man's hand. A slow-motion repeat would be best. I imagine it took a lot of practice. Plus, remind me not to make you angry."

Judging by how fast he spoke, Bruce still had adrenaline coursing through his veins. "Wait. You saw that happen? *You* were the one who shoved the paper out?"

He shrugged. "After I alerted the other deputy. I just wanted to cause a diversion, do something to help you. I know it wasn't much."

Her mouth dropped open. Did he think he had to protect her? How could he be confident in her ability to keep him and his daughter safe if he was worried about her needing help to do her job? "You also shoved me down when the gunmen approached us on the highway earlier. You can't do stuff like that, Bruce. You need to stay out of it."

"You can't expect me to stand idly by. What was I supposed to do, let them try to kill you?"

"Yes!" She threw her hands up in the air, but her cheeks heated. "That's exactly what I expect you to do," she said in a much softer voice. She wanted to tell him how much it meant to her that he cared enough to do something, but she couldn't. "It's my job to protect you, not the other way around."

Delaney had a point. He knew they probably didn't let untrained slackers into the Marshals, but it went against his every instinct to let Delaney defend him, even die for him. "That must've been in the fine print I skimmed," he said instead.

His father had taught him at a very young age to think of women first. It was old-fashioned, sure, but it was how he'd been raised. Whenever he went for a walk with his mom, he'd been taught to step to the outside to make sure he was the closest to the cars driving past. To be fair, his mom only allowed it if his dad was on the other side, also protecting him from traffic. The memory stuck, though. He knew being the protector was Delaney's job and after he'd witnessed her take down that gunman, he'd seen for himself that she was better trained for it. He might've made things worse by trying to help.

"Excuse me for a second." He walked to the bathroom and pulled back the shower curtain. "Found you." Winnie squealed and he reached down to pick her up and carry her back into the bedroom. "Okay, all done with that game. How about we get one of your toys out of our bag?"

Winnie jumped from his arms and onto the middle of the bed. Delaney stood in the open doorway between the connecting rooms, the duffel bag in her hand. "Is it a problem for you that I'm a woman?"

A problem for him to stop thinking about her? Yes, but that was probably not what she wanted to know. "Are you asking if I have a problem with a woman assigned as my protection detail?"

Her face scrunched up. She looked even cuter than when Winnie flashed the same expression. "What else would I mean?"

"No, Delaney." He sighed. He understood that Delaney was worried he'd step out of line again and try to protect her. He couldn't promise that his instincts wouldn't kick in, but he would try to stay out of her way as long as he could be of help from the sidelines. "You're competent and clearly well suited for your job. I'm sorry I tried to help. I'm not used to people trying to ki—" He pulled out a matching game for Winnie. "Well, you know."

Her shoulders dropped. "I do know. I'm not really upset with you. I'm angry that you were ever put in this position in the first place."

"You and me both. Where are our uninvited *guests* now anyway?" he asked.

Delaney's fists were curled at her sides, but she looked at Winnie and relaxed her fingers. "One of them got away," she said in a lighthearted voice. "So we sent some men to find him."

Winnie looked up. "Hide-and-seek?"

"Yes…sort of. Except these men were naughty. They didn't follow the rules."

"They were naughty? Did they go in time-out?"

Delaney looked as if she'd choked on something for half a second. "I guess you could call it a final time-out for the one who didn't get away." She shook her head and gave Bruce a pleading look. "I'm not good at this, at wording it differently."

Winnie went back to her game. Bruce held a hand out toward her. "You satisfied her curiosity."

Delaney blew out a heavy breath and addressed Bruce. "One *guest* down, if you know what I mean. Another was injured but managed to exit via the vending hallway."

Bruce hitched a thumb over his shoulder. "The shots I heard?"

"I think most of those came from our side, but yes." She nodded gravely. "We wanted a safe location with many exits to get you out quickly. Unfortunately, it sometimes means more access points for unfriendlies, as well. We had police covering them all, but our...*company* had identification that matched real FBI agents in the computer system. The police even called to verify them as real agents with the Bureau."

"Who is Kurt?" The question flew out of his mouth without much thought, but it'd been driving him crazy the past few minutes. "I noticed in the other room that you wrote 'What would Kurt do?'"

Her eyebrows rose. "Oh. Kurt is a fellow deputy marshal, a mentor really. I used to work with him in Coeur d'Alene. I learned a lot from him during my time there." She shook her head and stared at the carpet. "I'm afraid I sometimes doodle what I'm thinking. It's a bad habit."

"It's a habit of creative thinkers." He raised a hand. "Fellow doodler. Were you and he...? I mean, it's none of my business. I think I'm starting to feel the effects of isolation." He sank onto the edge of the mattress. Winnie took the opportunity to lunge for his neck and hang on his back like a monkey.

"We weren't a couple, if that's what you mean." Her shoulders relaxed and she smiled. Such a small thing made the world seem less dangerous. When she smiled her whole face lit up. "In fact, on the first case I worked with Kurt, he went and fell in love with his witness protectee." Her back and neck stiffened and her lips clamped shut, as if she couldn't believe she'd admitted it aloud.

Bruce's throat felt a little dry. "Is that common?" His attempt at acting nonchalant backfired. Even Winnie noticed, making a face at him as she abandoned him as a jungle gym and returned to her matching game.

"Uh...no." Her cheeks turned a lovely shade of pink. She looked down at her empty hands as if something should have been there. "I don't have the statistics in front of me, but I don't think it's common."

"But you're not sure?"

The pink flamed to crimson. "A marshal has to know a lot about the person they're protecting. And it's only natural that the witness would want some reciprocity to know about their assigned protector." She moved her hands to her hips, crossed her arms and finally dropped them at her sides. "I mean, not that you want reciprocity, just some...some witnesses do. So the marshal and the protectee sometimes do get to know each other fairly well. But it's not common for a romance to blossom. I'm sure, now that I say it aloud. Definitely not."

He frowned hard, so as not to outright laugh. "So,

in the case of Kurt and his witness, was it Stockholm syndrome?"

"No!" Her eyes widened and her mouth dropped. "I didn't kidnap you, Bruce." She leaned up against the door frame. "You're not trapped here. It would be foolish of you, but you can leave and go back home anytime you want."

"I want to go home," Winnie said.

Delaney placed a hand over her mouth for a second before dropping it. "Oh, I'm so sorry."

Bruce couldn't take his eyes off Delaney. He didn't want their conversation to end—talking to her filled him with sparks of electricity that made him feel alive again. But Winnie needed his attention right now.

He turned to his daughter. "Sweetheart, we can't go yet. We get to visit some more places first."

She shrugged. "Okay."

He turned back, relieved she'd been put off so easily. Experience had taught him that probably wouldn't be the case the next time. "So what did you decide Kurt would do?"

She tilted her head and frowned for a moment. Her eyes cleared and she looked directly at him. "Know the enemy."

SIX

The answer seemed so clear now. Bruce and Winnie would never be safe until she learned more about how the criminal organization worked, how they hunted their prey. Once she had all the facts, she could approach their protection more proactively. All it took was a small spark of hope to regain her focus.

"No one has even told me which hacking organization they suspect was behind Andy's—" Pain washed over his face.

Delaney wanted to yell at the Assistant US Attorney for skipping procedural steps. If she had Bruce's file, she'd know exactly what he witnessed without having to ask him. Delaney only knew the basics of Bruce's testimony. He'd walked in on the hacking and had notified security. Then he had seen the security guard be killed. But all the details were missing. She hadn't been fully briefed, and neither had Bruce—they'd just been thrown in together.

Although, if the attorney had waited any longer to send protection, Bruce and his daughter might've been dead by now.

"You should've been briefed," she said, "but since

the attempt at a pretrial meeting went horribly wrong, I don't think it's out of line to tell you what little I know. The suspected cybercriminal group that we believe is behind the attacks stays under the radar, though in law enforcement circles they're pretty well known. They call themselves the CryptTakers, but I don't know much more than that about them."

He exhaled. "Thanks for telling me." Bruce moved to one of the wingback chairs on the left side of the round table next to the closed curtains. "What do you want to know about them?"

She frowned. "Are you asking to help me think it through? Or you already familiar with the CryptTakers?"

"The latter. I'm pretty familiar with most hacking groups. But, if it helps, I'd be glad to help you think things through, as well. I'm pretty good at out-of-the-box thinking, and I've been told I'm good listener."

She pulled up the chair opposite him. "You didn't say anything earlier."

His eyes twinkled. "I don't like to brag."

She fought against rolling her eyes. "Not about your listening skills. You know about most hacking groups? You know about the CryptTakers?"

He held up both hands and rolled his eyes. "This is the first I've heard about the CryptTakers being involved. Why would I bring something like that up out of the blue?"

So he was human after all. If she'd been in his situation, she'd be irritated and grumpy all the time, but Bruce had, until this moment, constantly focused on the positive. The trait grated, partly because she used to be accused of the same thing. "Like I told you from the start, there's been an accelerated timeline and we're playing catch-up. You can rest assured the US Attorney's Office knows exactly who they're dealing with."

Bruce placed his elbows on his knees and rested his forehead on his fists. "Okay. Stop me if I'm telling you what you already know. Everything the CryptTakers do is for money. There's no Robin Hood mentality, political alliance or moral boundaries for this group."

"You're not telling me anything new so far. The group stays pretty hush-hush. You don't see them listed by name in the news."

"I'm a programmer. I need to know what I'm up against, especially seeing as banks use my software. At one point in my life, I considered becoming an ethical hacker. I even started a group and launched a competition when I was a student at Iowa State. It drew corporate sponsorship every year—still does—because businesses need good guys to help them find weaknesses before cybercriminals do."

"You used to be a hacker?"

"Back in the day, yes. I'm out of practice."

She tilted her head. "Did you know people in the CryptTakers?"

"I don't know who's involved with them so I can't say for sure, but that organization is more recent than my time in school, so I doubt there would be any overlap."

"Did you ever have to kick people out for unethical behavior? People that may have taken the way of groups like the CryptTakers?"

"Not really. We started by volunteering our time at some of the biggest companies, and if we found a weakness, we'd let the business know. No one was making money off of it—we saw it as a community service. The worst thing I can say about anyone is that if a company didn't take our suggestion under advisement, some members of our group thought it was their duty to release the vulnerability to the dark web."

"What do you know about the dark web?" she asked.

"It's essentially an online marketplace for drugs, money laundering…"

"I know that much, but I'm not as familiar with details."

"Well, the name says it all. It's where you can buy things that a legitimate vendor would never sell, which means it's where groups like CryptTakers get their assignments. They work using cloud technology to communicate, so it's pretty much impossible to shut it down."

"So you know how they work and how they think." The information gave her a better framework of who they were up against, but she wasn't dialed into this world and didn't know enough about how they operated. She needed practical tips to keep them safe. Her focus was drawn to the closed hotel door. She'd almost died. Her insides still fluttered from the near miss. A dead man was in the hallway. One more wrong move and Bruce and Winnie might've been killed, as well.

"How are they finding us?" Her voice shook ever so slightly, but she hoped Bruce hadn't noticed.

He pointed to the screen behind her. "If that's a smart television, they could hack into it to watch and listen to us if they wanted. A group like CryptTakers is going to find the technology on your phone, no matter how secure you say the Marshals made it. Electronic locks, newer vehicles, any devices…" He let his voice drift off. "They can get us through all of it. We need to think like our grandparents."

She grabbed a blanket from the closet and threw it over the television. "I don't follow."

"The only way we're going to stay hidden is if we go old-school. Literally."

"Old-school." She let her voice trail off, detailing a mental list of what that would involve. Where could they go to be cut off from all new technology? "It's a good thing you're already packed. I want to get back on the road as soon as the other deputies clear the perimeter."

Four hours and a ridiculous amount of phone calls later, Delaney pulled a crusty old moving van into the basement parking garage. Deputies waited for her in the pickup truck and an ancient Jeep parked on either side. Gone were the smartphones. It was imperative that everyone on her team knew the area well because their flip phones were without web and navigation capabilities.

She opened the car door and the humidity, without air-conditioning, hit her like a heavy, wet blanket. Bruce picked up a sleeping Winnie from the car seat and stepped out. Little ringlets stuck to the side of Winnie's face that wasn't pressed against Bruce. "Where to?" he whispered.

She threw his duffel bag, as well as hers, over her shoulder. Deputy Sanders hopped out of the passenger side of the pickup truck and took the keys from Delaney before getting behind the wheel. Bruce arched an eyebrow and watched as all three vehicles left the parking garage.

"Sorry. They're serving as decoys. One more small trip." In the corner of the parking garage a boxy vehicle waited underneath a tarp. She pulled the beige cover off.

"A golf cart?"

In any other situation, she would've laughed at his re-action. "It's as old-school as you get." She unzipped the clear door of the four-wall enclosure that allowed pas-sengers to ride inside despite sideways rain or whatever weather Iowa had to offer on any given summer day.

She placed the duffel bags in the back. The key was underneath the visor, just as the owner had said it would be. As soon as her protection detail was over, she would lecture him about theft prevention.

A friend of a friend on the force owned the golf cart and the network of apartment buildings. While he never intended any of them to be used as safe houses, Delaney knew from a football party years ago that the owner never sold the model apartment unit that was used as a showroom, even if all the other units were full. He liked to keep the furnished space reserved for guests and entertaining. As such, the apartment was tastefully decorated, but standard amenities such as a television, which she'd asked to be removed prior to their arrival, internet and phones would be nonexistent in the three-bedroom unit.

She drove the golf cart up the ramp, past the several other levels of the parking garage, until they reached the top floor.

"Is this where we'll be staying? Or do we have a hang glider waiting to take us to a different building?"

Delaney fought a laugh as she unlocked the main door. "You jest, but it sounds like a good idea to me." They walked down the empty, carpeted hallway until they reached 7A. She stuck the key into the lock. "Tomorrow will hopefully be the beginning of the end." She replayed the words that came out of her mouth and realized they could be interpreted the wrong way. The clock would strike midnight in less than five minutes, and apparently her brain was in the process of turning into a pumpkin. "I mean—"

A tired smile crossed his lips. "I know what you meant, Delaney. For better or worse, I think you're right."

"Either way, it's time for some sleep," Bruce added.

"No sleep." Winnie's head popped off his shoulder, her eyes wide. Great. It was if she'd had another three-hour nap. Her schedule was so messed up.

Bruce's own eyes were beginning to burn from lack of sleep. "Almost-three-year-olds aren't meant to go on the run."

"Is that what she needs to do? Run off the energy and try again?"

Winnie wiggled in his arms, but he held on and didn't let her down. "Toddlers, despite being so lightweight, somehow sound like an elephant stampede when they run. Aren't there people living below this floor?"

The door at the opposite end of the hallway opened. Before he could blink, Delaney's gun was at her side, pointed at the carpet, and the keys were left dangling from the lock. A man who easily had five inches on Bruce stepped in the light, wearing jeans and a T-shirt with an olive green backpack slung over his shoulder. He raised his left hand.

Delaney mirrored the greeting and reholstered the gun. "That's Officer McCollins. He's actually the reason we were able to get the entire top floor. He knows the owner." The man made no move to approach them. He slid a key into the door at the opposite end of the hall and entered with another wave. "I don't envy him.

Not only did he hike from his house to make sure no one followed, but that unit is unfurnished."

"Doesn't anyone live on this floor?"

She returned to the door and opened it. "The entire level is considered the penthouse because it's the only floor that has access to the roof, so all the units here are substantially more pricey. It's all ours." Her back straightened. "Actually, the roof would be the perfect place for Winnie to run off some energy before you try to get her to sleep again."

She threw the duffel bags on the suede couch inside the open living area. "There are three bedrooms here, so when we get back we can each have one. We'll have another officer hike in shortly to take the sofa bed." She grabbed her walkie-talkie and alerted McCollins where they were going. "Follow me. It's the highest building in the area so we should be safe from any eyes."

Despite the exhaustion, he followed her upstairs to a door at the top that required a key. "I'm not so sure I want her to run on the roof. That sounds dangerous."

"Just wait and see." Delaney opened the final door and flicked a light switch. A four-foot wall wrapped around the roof. Strings of lights attached on the borders cast dim but adequate light onto the flat structure. Camp chairs leaned up against the side wall next to the door. As far as Bruce could tell, there was no way Winnie could climb the wall. He set Winnie down. "Okay. You can run around."

"Look at the Christmas lights, Daddy."

"They're pretty, but they're not for Christmas. It's still summer."

Winnie ran with her arms out and squealed in delight before she spun around. Bruce laughed. "I'm not sure an entire floor in between us and sleeping tenants will be enough."

"I'm sure enough for both of us." Delaney crossed her arms, looking pleased. "I went to a party once here. I don't remember why, but they shot off fireworks from the game." Bruce looked over and spotted Jack Trice Stadium, partly lit up by the parking lot lights surrounding it.

"You had a great view from here."

She smiled as if seeing the game all over again. "We did."

"I haven't been to a game in ages."

"Too busy?"

"It seems selfish to leave Winnie with a babysitter after a week in day care to go cheer for some guys fighting over a ball." The words didn't ring true. He used to love watching the Cyclones, but he didn't even allow himself that indulgence at home these days, even though Winnie's nap often overlapped a game during fall weekends. So focused on doing everything right, even more so since his marriage to Shannon and partnership with Trevor had gone so wrong, he wasn't even sure he'd enjoy it anymore.

"Well, I wouldn't know about that." Her chin jutted out as she stressed each word. Either she didn't want to be a parent or the sudden change in demeanor had something to do with the past.

"If you don't mind me asking, why did you move away from here?" he asked.

Her eyebrows jumped. "The short answer is that I decided to join the Marshals."

Winnie hopped from one rubber square to the next. "Seems we have time for the long answer."

Delaney glanced at him, her eyebrows raised, as if shocked he'd dared to ask.

He laughed. "I believe you said it's only natural for a witness to want to know more about their assigned protector. It's true I'm at a disadvantage. You know a lot about me."

She broke into a sheepish smile. "I set myself up for that one, didn't I?" She shook her head. "Well, it's not the happiest story. I actually lost someone."

He'd suspected as much ever since that ride in the back seat of the police cruiser. And somehow, late at night, with the stars as a backdrop, it seemed the right time to ask. "From the force?"

"Yes. There was an accident, and he died instantly. He was actually best friends with Officer McCollins." She turned and faced away from him. "That's how I knew about this place."·

"I'm so sorry." His voice was almost a whisper. Winnie seemed to be affected by the quiet of the night as she collected leaves that the wind had deposited. "Was he your—"

"We were engaged. Well, unofficially. Looking back, I don't know if he was dragging his feet because he was scared or just felt obligate—" Her shoulders pulled back. "Don't want to bore you with details. I took a leave of absence and decided the Marshals was the place for me."

Something stirred inside his chest. Her words didn't give him many specifics, but he saw in her the same expression he had worn after Shannon left. Had Delaney been left with the same question of whether she'd ever been loved? Her words seemed to hint at the question. "Do you mind me asking why the Marshals? You could've transferred to another police department, right?"

"I needed a new challenge, something I could give my all. I felt, personally, more freedom to make a difference in the Marshals. Turns out, I'm good at tracking fugitives. I didn't need to worry about collecting evidence or investigating crimes, I just needed to find the escapees and bring them in."

"Is that what you'd rather be doing now?"

She spun around to face him. "I'm good at protecting witnesses, too, Bruce. It's just not as easy of an assignment. Hear me when I say that we haven't lost a single witness who complied with WITSEC."

"Except you said this wasn't WITSEC."

She winced. "You're right, I did. But the point is you're safe."

"You're trying to prepare me for a move to WITSEC, aren't you?"

"I always prefer to plan for contingencies, the worst-case scenarios, just in case." Her kind eyes met his. "I assume other people would prefer that, as well."

He breathed in slowly. If it came down to the point where he'd need to enter WITSEC, he didn't know if he'd be able to go through with testifying. Saying goodbye to his business, raising Winnie with a different name, on less money, still alone with no one to trust... He couldn't do it.

"Bruce."

She said his name tentatively, as if easing him into bad news. He knew that tone and tensed, prepared for the worst. "Yes?"

"I really do think we have a solid, safe plan lined up for the morning. This time it'll be different, but..."

"I'm not changing my mind about Winnie, if that's what you're asking. I won't testify unless she goes where I go. I'm not leaving her with anyone I don't trust explicitly, no offense to the other marshals. I want the best protecting her and since you're leading my detail, I assume you're the best. If you can protect me, you can protect Winnie because they'll have to kill me to get to her."

Delaney kicked at a loose piece of gravel. "Understood."

The sounds of cicadas in the distance calmed his thoughts.

"You mentioned that you go to church weekly," she said. "I hope I'm not out of line to say I hope you're praying right now." She looked up and the moonlight lit up her eyes. "I don't want to give you the wrong impression. I'm confident we will keep you and your daughter safe, but I'm also a believer and wondered if knowing that would help you feel better, since where two or more are gathered—"

"Absolutely." He reached down and held her hand. She flinched at first, before her fingers wrapped around his knuckles. The softness of her touch flustered his thoughts for a moment. "Let's pray." He bent his head down and whispered a short plea for safety and peace, and the most pressing need at the moment, sleep.

While Delaney said nothing, she gave his hand a squeeze, which he'd learned in the past year was the unofficial sign of agreement at the end of a prayer. He let go, though he'd be lying to himself if he didn't admit he hesitated. Their fingers slid slowly apart. Was she hesitating, too? And, for that matter, was she lying to herself and to him about how safe tomorrow's travel plan would be?

She blew out a breath and swatted at a flying nuisance that he could only assume was a mosquito. "I'd hoped we were high enough to avoid being bit."

"I've heard they can still thrive in high-rise buildings. And on that note, I think it's time to call it a night." The last thing he needed was a hyper toddler who had itchy bites. "Winnie."

His little girl ignored him. "Winona Olivia Walker, come here now."

Winnie froze, her eyes comically wide. Bruce rarely ever used her full name because he never wanted her to get so used to it that she lost that priceless reaction when he did.

"It's time to go," he said in a softer voice.

She sauntered, arms swinging wide, in a slow walk. He met her halfway and scooped her into his arms.

"I'm tired." She rubbed her eyes for emphasis.

Never had there been sweeter words. "Let's go to sleep, then." He followed Delaney back down the stairs, forcing himself to believe the worst of the danger would be over after tomorrow, despite every fiber of his being screaming otherwise.

SEVEN

Despite the exhaustion, the comfortable bed and an additional officer posted in the living room during the night shift, Delaney had maybe slept all of half an hour before her door creaked open. She flung her covers back as she sat upright.

Winnie stood in the hallway, her hand on the doorknob. "Lights out." She ran into the room and jumped onto Delaney's bed. The comfort Winnie exhibited in being close to Delaney ripped off another protective layer of her heart.

"My lights *are* out." Delaney pointed to the lamp on the nightstand.

Winnie pointed to the curtains where a weak stream of sunlight leaked in. Ah, so she meant that it was light outside. "Does your daddy know you're in here?"

"Daddy's sleeping." She pursed her lips and raised her eyebrows as if Delaney should be scandalized by the information.

"Okay." The clock read six in the morning, and while she'd hoped to sleep until seven, some extra time to get her thoughts gathered on such a big day wouldn't be a bad thing. Despite her confidence in the travel plan, she hated not knowing exactly how the gunmen had found them the past two times.

Bruce had said he wanted the best deputy to protect them. *Please help me be the best.* It was the first time she'd ever prayed such a thing without a competitive spirit.

The little girl kept smiling at her. Winnie gave her hope. Hope that her own adopted girl was happy and smiling somewhere out there. Delaney blinked back the moisture collecting in her eyes. "If you wait here for a minute while I get ready, we'll get you some breakfast. I'll try to be super fast."

Delaney stepped inside the attached bathroom to wash her face, brush her teeth and change into the postal uniform she'd be wearing for the day. Thankfully, she'd showered the night before, but her hair was its usual wavy, unmanageable mess. She slipped on a nondescript blue hoodie over the uniform as the air-conditioning kicked on. A small knock at her door meant time was up.

Delaney opened it and Winnie stepped inside with a shrug of her shoulders. "Whatcha doin'?"

A wave of fondness almost knocked Delaney over. She battled the same thought that had kept her tossing and turning all night. Olivia was Winnie's middle name. Delaney had almost demanded to know why Bruce had made her middle name Olivia. Logically, it had to be a coincidence. It was one of the more popular girl's names, but Olivia had also been the name Delaney had chosen for her baby. In a burst of emotion at the hospital, she'd asked Harvey Jeppsen if he could suggest it to the adopting parents.

Winnie reached over and grabbed Delaney's brush off the countertop. "I'll do your hair."

"That's okay." Delaney reached out to take it back, but Winnie hid it behind her back and gave her a look Delaney felt certain meant screaming if Delaney didn't comply. "Okay, then. I guess you can do my hair."

Delaney pointed to the hallway and led Winnie to the living room, where she excused the officer who looked ready to fall asleep. He waved goodbye and Winnie took his place on the couch as Delaney started a fresh pot of coffee. "What do you like for breakfast?"

"I like cheesy eggs."

Delaney had thought for sure the answer would be doughnuts or waffles, but eggs seemed surprisingly sensible. She picked up her radio and asked Officer McCollins to arrange for a bacon, egg and cheese biscuit delivery.

With nothing else to do, Delaney sat down. Winnie scooted next to her and proceeded to brush her hair, if it could be called that. Winnie shoved the brush into her hair and pulled down forcefully. Delaney cried out before she could stop herself.

Bruce burst into the hallway. He stilled and took in the scene of them on the couch. Delaney's cheeks burned. "She wanted to brush my hair," she explained.

Winnie left the hairbrush dangling in Delaney's locks but leaned over so that their faces were almost touching. She held up her own hair next to Delaney's. They blended perfectly. It was almost enough to make Delaney cry out again.

Bruce laughed, shaking his head. "She's a force to be reckoned with in the morning before she's had her breakfast. Winnie, you were supposed to wake Daddy up first."

A knock at the door prompted Delaney to leap to her feet. She checked to see who it was before working the tangled hairbrush out of her hair. Officer McCollins held a fast-food bag full of breakfast. She accepted and handed it to an eager Bruce and Winnie, who both devoured their meals without complaint.

"Do children her age normally talk so much?"

"No." The emphasis on the word was so strong it was all she could do not to laugh.

"She's precocious." He grinned at Winnie. "Started talking in full sentences at eighteen months."

What Delaney really wanted to do was ask him all sorts of details about Winnie's adoption, just to put her mind at ease. She'd been able to put every other fleeting suspicion to rest, but the Olivia thing still rattled her thinking. What if Winnie didn't know she was adopted? Delaney would need to wait until she had a minute alone with Bruce to ask. "Hold on." The realization hit her all at once and she couldn't help but burst out, "Winnie Olivia Walker. Her initials are WOW?"

He chuckled. "Yes. On purpose."

She frowned. While the information she had on him was minimal, she knew his middle name was Otis. "And your initials are…"

"BOW. Yes. Together, we are BOWWOW." His grin took her breath away. "That part wasn't intentional."

She gulped down coffee and took a few bites of her sandwich. It was time to get her head in the game. "About Winnie…"

"I consider myself flexible, but my daughter isn't up for discussion. She stays with me."

"I was going to say I don't have an outfit for her." She pulled out a postal uniform and handed it to him. "Only one for you. But consider yourself warned. It's not going to be the most comfortable ride for either of you."

He grumbled but shuffled off to his room. A few minutes later he stepped out in the postal outfit. The blue shirt and the navy shorts didn't look terrible on him, but the white socks pulled up to his shins along with the black shoes had a certain comical quality. She clamped her jaw shut to keep from laughing.

"It looks like a dad outfit," he said.

"Well, you are one." Delaney tried to be discreet as she slipped two guns into the postal mailbag before she slung the bag diagonally across her torso. "It's time to go."

Bruce had never considered himself a vain man, but the white socks and black shoes still got to him. His own dad, not one to care a bit about his public image, had worn a similar outfit on Sunday afternoons. It was one of the few memories he had of his father, since he'd passed away when Bruce was ten.

Would this moment be a memory Winnie held of him?

Hopefully she'd remember him as a man who did the right thing, fought for justice and made the best mac and cheese that didn't come from a blue box. Delaney handed him a navy cap and placed one on her own head, which looked adorable with her wavy hair draped through the back.

He glanced down at her shoes. "Hey. How come you get short navy socks and matching shoes? I think I'd like to file a complaint."

She shrugged. "I didn't pick out the clothes." She grinned at Winnie and their eyes seemed to twinkle at the same time. Their expressions looked so similar, it caught Bruce off guard for a second.

Winnie scrunched her nose up. "Daddy looks so funny." Her laughs, a little extra boisterous for his sake, grew louder.

He picked her up. "Are you ready to go in the mail truck? You want to pretend to be a letter?"

"No. I want to be a present."

"I agree. You are definitely the best present I've ever received."

He grabbed his own mock mailbag and placed all of Winnie's favorite items inside to help keep her busy in the truck and at the courthouse.

In the parking garage, a mail truck and two other package delivery vans waited. Delaney pointed at the other two drivers. "Remember. No radio unless necessary."

The metallic benches in the back of the postal vehicle had hooks where tethers to the car seat had been attached. Bruce sat on the bench opposite Winnie while Delaney sat in the driver's seat. The openness of the vehicle allowed him to hear her as easily as if he'd been sitting next to her.

"Be glad it's early. The windows are staying rolled up and there's no air-conditioning."

His heart beat faster as the truck sped down the parking ramps. *Let this time be different.* He felt a little more at peace, but it might've been self-assurance since he'd played a part in their travel plan by suggesting they use vehicles without vulnerable technology. The truck was so old it didn't have any way to be hacked, and after hearing Delaney explain that the Marshals used to deliver witnesses in mail trucks in the "olden days" of witness protection, it seemed a fitting way to travel.

Delaney didn't lean back into her seat, and from Bruce's vantage point, he could see that she was constantly glancing in all directions, alert for any signs of trouble.

Winnie settled in with an activity book, placing princess stickers all over the car seat, oblivious to the knots forming in her dad's stomach and neck. Without radio or conversation, the hum of traffic and the vibration from the tires on the road did little to quiet his mind. He wanted to talk to Delaney to get out of his own head, but he didn't want to distract her. The minutes crawled, interspersed with a few requests from Winnie for juice, a snack or more stickers.

The attorneys would want him to relive every detail of Max's death at the pretrial interview, and again at the trial, as if it didn't replay every time he closed his eyes. He didn't need any practice. Maybe the pretrial interview was more for the attorneys than him.

The radio crackled but Bruce couldn't make out the words. Delaney looked over her shoulder for a split second. "We're here but driving around the area until they're finished with the first witness."

"How is Mrs. King doing?" If he used Nancy's first name, Winnie would get hyped-up and start looking for her. It'd been a while since Winnie had had time with her honorary grandma.

"I don't get communication updates on anything more than her safety." The static returned and Delaney answered. "Two minutes. Over." The sound of the turn signal clicked on and off as she took a sharp right. The hum of the road changed. Bruce leaned forward as they crossed the bridge over the Des Moines River.

Fast approaching on the right-hand side, he spotted the stone building that housed the US District Courts. Delaney didn't slow down until she turned onto 2nd Street. Cars were parked along the side streets with few empty spots available. A fenced parking lot connected the stately courthouse and the glass-walled bankruptcy court on the other side.

She slowed the mail truck down to a crawl but passed by an electronic gate while looking in the opposite direction.

"There are trees on the other side. I'd rather use that gate since it offers more protection," Delaney explained, but Bruce wondered if she had seen something suspicious. She turned onto Walnut Street and stopped at the mailbox in front of the bankruptcy court for a brief second, opened and closed the box, most likely to keep up appearances. She sped around 1st Street to the gated entrance set between two oak trees.

She held out her hand, presumably holding a badge, to a black box and the black metal gate slid to the left in response. A man stepped into the sunlight in the parking lot. He spotted the mail truck and turned in a way that kept the woman behind him blocked from view. "That has to be Nancy," Bruce said.

Delaney smiled. "Her appointment is over. It's your turn."

"Nancy?" Winnie perked up, hopeful.

A shot rang out and the deputy lurched forward, blood spraying upward. Another shot and Nancy crumpled. Screams rang out from the courthouse steps and uniformed men ran out from the safety of the overhang, hunched beside cars, looking up, weapons in hand. The drivers from their escort vehicles ran through the gate, toward the danger.

Bruce reeled as the mail truck spun backward. A metal crunching sound reverberated through the truck. "Have we been hit?"

"Everyone okay?" Delaney shouted at the same time. He had a feeling the truck had been shot at, but he didn't see where the bullet had landed. Bruce launched himself out of his seat and sat next to Winnie, both shielding her and frantically checking for any injuries. Her activity book had fallen out of her hands and slid to the back of the truck.

Delaney picked up her radio and spoke rapidly. "Shots fired. Two down. Origin appeared to be roof of the southeast building across street. Walnut and 1st. Two hundred yards from victims. Over."

Bruce groaned, hung his head and kissed Winnie's forehead, all while praying for protection for Winnie, Nancy and the deputies. Someone had been waiting for them.

The radio blared with affirmations that the Marshals were after the shooter. Orders were directed at other deputies until a man's voice shouted, "Delaney! The quiet place. Do you understand? Go to the quiet place! Alone."

Delaney didn't waste a second. She hit the gas and sped down the street. A moment later, she took another sharp turn. Winnie's eyes filled with unshed tears as she released a shaky laugh, unsure whether the wild ride was supposed to be fun or scary or both. The reaction broke his heart. He'd brought her with him to protect her, not to put her in more danger. He kept his arms and body around her car seat, as close as he could manage. "It's okay, honey. Daddy is here, and Delaney is taking us somewhere safe." The lack of air-conditioning was taking its toll. Winnie's hair hung limp and her cheeks looked flushed.

"The quiet place. Where's that?"

Delaney swerved around a car on the bridge. "I honestly have no idea."

"We need the windows open. It's getting too hot."

"Agreed. Give me five minutes."

Five more minutes... Did Nancy have five more minutes of life left? Or had she died instantly? Nancy was more than an honorary grandmother. She'd been his right hand, his encourager and a friend. First Max, now Nancy. When would it stop? If they kept going, would he see Winnie meet the same fate? Bruce fought tears at the thought.

Raising Winnie in the witness protection program had been his biggest fear, but the moment the deputy and Nancy hit the ground, a new worry took first place. He'd do anything to keep Winnie safe, and while he couldn't walk away from the case without justice for Max, and now Nancy, his concerns about starting over with Winnie seemed trivial.

Saying goodbye to his identity was a price he was finally willing to pay. But his heart still ached at the thought of it. Disappearing from the lives of the people he cared about and the life he'd built would be painful. Bruce glanced at Delaney. The hardest part about leaving would be saying goodbye and knowing he'd never see her, and everyone else, again.

EIGHT

The quiet place? Delaney drove across the river, searching for any kind of clue or escape, all the while checking
to make sure they weren't being followed.

They needed a new vehicle right away, preferably one
better equipped. She cracked the windows but didn't
roll them all the way down. It wasn't safe for Winnie
to drive much farther without air-conditioning with the
temperature and humidity increasing by the hour. How
far would they be driving? She had no idea—not a single
notion of where to go. The quiet place... What could
he have meant?

Never before had she realized how much she relied
on technology. Delaney made fun of people who kept
their heads bent down in unnatural positions all day
long, staring at their phone screens. To be fair, she kept
her head down for large periods of time as well, but
only because she had a voracious appetite for devour-
ing books, which was totally different.

She knew the Ames region like the back of her hand,
but Des Moines wasn't as fresh, though she'd spent
much of her free time there in high school and college.

If she found a familiar landmark, maybe it would all come back to her.

Sirens blared and an ambulance passed by so fast she wouldn't have had time to pull over to the side of the road even if she'd wanted. Were they going to help the courthouse victims?

The way the deputy and the witness had collapsed in the parking lot attempted to replay in her mind. Her training kicked in and she breathed deeply and purposely relaxed her shoulders. The small changes helped her focus on the present moment.

A sign pointed in the direction of a hospital up ahead to the left. Her mouth dropped at the sight of the building that sat kitty-corner. She whispered a prayer of thanks and slipped into the employee parking lot of the United States Postal Service, right in between four other mail trucks.

She dropped her head onto the steering wheel for a brief second until she realized that might appear to Bruce as if she'd given up hope. She straightened up and prayed with her eyes open as she glanced around the facility. *Give me wisdom about the quiet place.*

The man with the gruff voice who'd issued the command over the radio had to be her former police chief—now US Marshal Bradford. A vague memory of him sitting in a chair next to her hospital bed, when she was in recovery after her emergency surgery, came into focus. He'd told her that when he had bypass surgery he'd found he needed to get out of the house while recovering to keep his head on straight. He'd recommended a visit to Reiman Gardens.

No offense, Chief, she'd told him, *but I don't think I'm going to want to be around other people.* She'd kept her eyes closed so she wouldn't cry in front of him anymore. He'd already seen her torn apart so much in the past few weeks.

Which is exactly why you need to be around them, Bradford had answered. *Not to talk to other people. Just to be present. Remind yourself that there is a world out there, and you're still a part of it. There are a couple benches on the west side, out of the way of foot traffic, among trees and flowers and birds. It's still my favorite quiet place.*

She felt her eyes widen and spun around in her seat. "I know where the quiet place is. Get her out of the car seat. I'll secure a ride." Reiman Gardens would also be the last place that anyone would suspect they'd go, as long as they didn't leave a digital footprint.

Bruce wiped away the thin layer of perspiration from his forehead. "Hopefully the next vehicle has air-conditioning."

"As long as the CryptTakers can't figure out our origin point, we can use a more updated car, right?"

"Yes." His fingers worked to disable the many latches holding Winnie inside the seat. "How did they find us in the first place?"

Would it discourage him even more if she told him she had no idea? "All I can figure is they knew you and—" she glanced at Winnie and made sure to omit Nancy's name "—the other witness would have to go to the court sooner or later."

"I find it hard to believe that someone has been waiting and watching the courthouse this entire time without one of the marshals noticing. They couldn't just watch remotely with electronic surveillance, because they'd have to be there to act as soon as one of us arrived."

She shared the same doubt, but she didn't know how else to explain it unless they had a mole among one of the court employees or within the US Attorney's Office. It could even be an unintentional leak. No matter the amount of training and policies, people still made mistakes. The Marshals tried to account for human error in their protection detail plans but maybe she needed to face facts that they were no match for the CryptTakers. At least *she* wasn't. If she could get Bruce to Reiman Gardens, she'd ask Bradford for a new deputy to be assigned as lead, someone more experienced.

Another postal truck pulled up and a woman in her late fifties with curly blond hair and kind eyes stepped out of the vehicle. "Stay here a minute," Delaney said. She hopped out of the truck and smiled at the lady. "I'm new here, and it turns out my friend isn't able to pick me up for lunch. I'm wondering if you'd be able to give me a quick ride?"

"You need a personal fan."

"Excuse me?"

The lady pointed at her hair. "That's what I call wet noodle hair. Sure sign of a rookie, but don't you worry. I hear we're getting new trucks soon with both heat and air. The prototypes have been seen in Virginia." The woman blinked. "And I don't drive a car here, hon. I take the bus."

"The bus?" Iowa had a network of bus systems and if she remembered correctly, there was a regular route from Des Moines to Iowa State University. "Where is the closest stop?"

She pointed over Delaney's shoulder. "Right across the street at the hospital."

Delaney smiled. "Thank you." She said it aloud, intending her gratitude for the Lord as much as the lady. She stepped back into her truck, and as soon as the lady had gone inside the mailroom, she waved Bruce forward. "Leave the car seat." She knew from her time as a police officer that most public buses didn't have seat belts or lower latches for installation.

She took off the postal cap she wore and gestured for Bruce to also hand his over. The knife on her multi-tool keychain made short work of the patch. It left holes in the hat, but if someone were to drive by on the street, they wouldn't notice. "Put it back on and keep it low over your eyes. Flip open the mailbag flap so no one can see the USPS logo and sling it across your chest so it mostly covers up the post office logo on your shirt. And fold those ridiculous socks down so they semi resemble crew socks."

She drew in a deep breath while Bruce sprang into action without complaint.

She turned to Winnie. "Sweetheart, is it okay if I hold you?" On the street, she and Winnie needed to look like a mom and daughter out and about instead of a deputy packing heat and a child under protection. With Winnie draped over her, it would be hard to tell she was wearing a postal uniform. Bruce simply needed to look alone and keep his face as covered as possible.

Winnie surprised Delaney by reaching her arms out for her. Her little body was like a giant hot-water bottle. The humidity made Delaney's clothes moist and sticky, and the little girl radiated heat, too.

Bruce straightened and the small modifications he'd made to his clothes served their purpose.

"We're headed for the hospital. Let's go." She purposefully walked closer than normal to a family on the sidewalk that was about to cross the street, in hopes she and Winnie looked like part of the group.

The walk sign illuminated. Delaney shifted Winnie to her opposite hip and stepped in front of Bruce so she would be the only one exposed to traffic, one hand ready to grab her weapon. They needed to look like different people to blend into the public, but she wasn't about to stop taking her job seriously.

She stepped to the side of one of four bus stops that surrounded the medical complex and peeked at the schedule. Perfect. Their ride would arrive in twenty minutes, which meant they had time for another wardrobe change. "Who wants to go clothes shopping at the hospital?"

Bruce assumed that when Delaney said they were changing clothes, they would do a cloak-and-dagger maneuver where he'd end up walking out in a surgeon's scrubs. And maybe that was the plan after all. Delaney didn't share with him what she had in mind as she sat them down in a waiting room on the second floor and then headed off on her own.

At first, he'd guessed she'd chosen the location because it was the safest place for them to linger, but the waiting room was also quite far from the emergency entrance. Did Delaney want to keep them from seeing Nancy covered in blood? Or was it because she wouldn't be there? Had they taken her straight to the morgue?

Winnie ran from empty chair to empty chair, tapping the seat covers as if in the middle of an invisible game of tag. Shaking off his morbid thoughts, he focused hard on the contagious joy pouring from his daughter.

He blinked and realized Delaney was standing in

front of him. He'd be lying if he said he wasn't disappointed when she held up a green T-shirt with the hospital logo on the pocket. She'd already changed into a maroon polo with the same emblem.

She frowned. "The green doesn't exactly go with the navy shorts and black shoes, but it's better than nothing." She pointed to the restroom before she hitched a thumb over her shoulder. "We've got ten minutes to get to the bus." She slipped a bag full of snacks into the mailbag he'd left on a chair. He sped through the motions of changing and met them back in the hallway.

"We look like off duty hospital employees."

"Don't flatter yourself. We look like volunteers here for orientation, and if anyone asks, that's what we just did today. Let's move."

Bruce had never noticed before that people rarely looked each other in the eye while walking the hospital halls. Delaney had no problem doing so, though. She smiled that radiant grin of hers at every person who passed, but he didn't miss how her hand moved casually from Winnie's back to her own waist. Someone else might have thought her lower back was starting to complain from the weight of the toddler but Bruce knew better. The outline of the gun's handle could barely be seen under the fabric of the untucked polo shirt.

At the corner, he strode forward to match her gait. Winnie had fallen asleep against her chest. "Let me take her," he said softly. "I want you to be able to use two hands if you need to aim."

"I promise I would've told you if I needed more than one." Delaney grinned and lifted Winnie into his grasp. She rose on her tiptoes and her arms slid along his to ensure Winnie stayed asleep during the handoff. Delaney looked up and her eyes widened as she met his gaze, as if she hadn't realized before that their lips were now only inches apart. Or maybe he was the only one thinking about their close proximity, and she was startled because she could see his thoughts written all over his face.

His stomach heated and he took a step back. "Thank you."

She bit her lip, nodded and resumed her stride in silence. They reached the bus stop just as the bus could be seen coming down University. "We'll have to change bus lines in Ames once, but it should be a smooth ride."

"I can't remember the last time I traveled without a phone. Is it sad that I keep reaching for my pocket, hoping it'll be there?"

She shook her head. "I think it's been at least five years since I've gone anywhere without one."

"Is that all?"

"Before that, I had a phone supplied by work, but I never carried it around for personal reasons until I was the last person without one. I hate to admit I thought it was a trend that would die."

"Yeah, different world now." The air brakes squeaked and hissed as the bus slowed to a stop, but amazingly, Winnie remained asleep. "Just how early was she in your room this morning?"

Delaney shook her head before waving him forward. "You don't want to know. You get on the bus first. I'll come up behind and pay. If it's available, take a middle row, or closest to it, on the left side when you're looking down the bus. And by the way, we're married for this trip."

That was a lot of details to digest. *Middle row. Left*

side. He stepped past her and glanced down at her hand. "No ring."

"Got out of the habit of wearing it when we had the baby. One scratch from the diamond, and I didn't want to risk hurting her again."

She said it so easily, as if she'd given it some thought. But how could she have?

The bus door finally opened, but he remained still. "And what about my missing ring?"

Delaney tilted her head. "A silent protest from you until I start wearing my ring again. Now, can you please get on the bus?"

He chuckled and began the ascent up the stairs. The bus driver appeared to be in his sixties, with a large mustache the likes of which Bruce had only seen on firefighters. "The wife is paying."

The driver and deputy didn't react. She leaned past him and held out the cash for the tickets. Assured everything was going as she expected, Bruce glanced at the other passengers. In the back were several young people. Young people? Since when did he call college students *young people*?

He'd never been the type to feel old until this week. Facing death and worry did that to a person. The thought reminded him of the way Nancy used to tease him about his young age. *Used to*. Even his thoughts had given up hope that she could have survived. His eyes burned. He needed more sleep.

Bruce held Winnie up higher so as not to bump the edges of seats as he passed them. He sank into the middle row on the left side, as Delaney had indicated. He shifted Winnie slightly so he could rest his elbow on the armrest and leaned his head back.

He felt Delaney sit down beside him but didn't open his eyes, still waiting for the sting to dissipate. "I would never be so passive-aggressive."

"What?" she asked.

He rubbed his forehead with his free hand before turning to her. "The ring thing. I would never react in silent protest when you were just trying to keep our child from getting hurt."

Her eyes widened before she crossed her legs. "Good to know," she said softly. If they hadn't been in danger, he wouldn't have thought twice about the casual way she shifted to look around the bus.

"Why'd you want me to sit here?" He kept his voice low, but there wasn't anyone sitting closer than three rows away. "Is there a reason, or does it just happen to be your favorite place to sit when you travel?"

"We're going north, so this side of the bus is farther away from oncoming traffic." She gestured forward and backward. "I have the best vantage point here with two exits to choose from, depending on the situation."

"So, it really is your favorite place to sit." He should've known she had reasons behind her decisions.

She turned to him and smiled. Every time Delaney did that it was like someone took a stick blender to his thoughts. Everything in his surroundings went all fuzzy except her pretty smile.

A small snore escaped from Winnie. He moved his arm ever so slightly so she was more upright. She twisted and leaned her head more on his chest than shoulder and resumed heavy breathing. His previous questions returned with the change of focus. Except Delaney still wore a smile, this one aimed at his daughter. She had really warmed up to Winnie in the last day.

He wondered what had brought on the change. Perhaps she'd liked kids all along but feared it made her look weak or less professional to show it. Maybe she was trying to take Winnie's feelings into account and discouraging any attachment, knowing her presence in their lives would be short-lived.

Or maybe he was the one who needed to be discouraged.

Her forehead scrunched. "Are you okay? Holding up?"

He wasn't falling apart outwardly, but he couldn't say the same inwardly. Too many feelings and thoughts demanded attention, and since he couldn't run or get on his phone or bury himself in a programming problem, the only way to cope was to focus on the people right in front of him.

He couldn't tell her that, though, because the natural reaction would be follow-up questions that would make him feel and think about issues neither one of them had answers or solutions for. Bruce needed to change the subject or ask more questions about her. "Do you always lie so easily?" The question blurted out of his mouth before he could stop it.

Her eyes widened. "Excuse me?"

"I mean with the ring story," he added hastily. "That came out wrong. I was just impressed with how fast you had solutions."

She faced forward, clasped her hands and looked down at her fingers. "I used to have a birthstone ring, an opal surrounded with little fake diamonds. I accidentally scratched a friend with it when I hugged them once. I don't know if that can happen with all rings, but I wondered."

"Still. It was fast thinking."

"I…uh…" She cast a side glance, then shook her head. "Never mind."

"No. You can't do that. Spill what you were going to say or I'll imagine the worst."

She shrugged. "It was nothing. I used to enjoy improv. It's been ages, but it was something I enjoyed."

"When did you do it?"

"Not since college really. ISU had an improv club."

"No kidding." He grinned. "I believe they still do. Did you ever participate in the theater productions?"

She seemed sheepish, which Bruce couldn't understand. Were law enforcement officials not supposed to have hobbies?

"I minored in theater. It's kind of an unusual mix with a criminal justice major, but I thought the development of a quick wit would be useful. Aside from roasting each other, I can't say it's really come in that handy yet, but I did act in one of the productions—*The Chronicles of Narnia*."

"Wow. Maybe that's why you look familiar."

Her mouth dropped. "Seriously? We were there at the same time? Did you see it?"

"I ran the lighting. It's all a computer-controlled system, you know." Man, he missed being behind a keyboard and screen. "Aside from my ethical hacking group and throwing javelin in track, serving as a theater lackey filled the rest of my free time."

Her features softened. "So we might have already met? Years ago? And you used to throw javelin?"

"Let's not say how many years, but it's likely we met. Though even now, I don't remember you in that setting. You must be a good singer. It was a musical, if I remember correctly." He wondered if her singing voice was that much different from her speaking voice. "Given the cruel and unusual avoidance of all entertainment and screen use, does protection detail include singing upon request?"

Her face turned the fiercest shade of red he'd ever seen. "Well…I haven't done that in quite some time. Besides, I bought you a sudoku book so you're not without entertainment. It's in the bag with the snacks." Her eyes narrowed. "Don't think I didn't notice how you avoided my initial question. How are you holding up?"

A level of weariness he hadn't known existed draped over his shoulders. "Do you think Nancy is dead?" His breathing grew shallow and the emotion he kept fighting jumped back to the front lines.

"I don't know how bad the initial injury was, but if it wasn't fatal, then I think she has a good chance. It only took me a minute to drive over the bridge, remember? You heard the sirens, I'm sure. The deputy marshals, court security officers and police were all on the scene. They would have secured the perimeter immediately so that by the time the ambulance reached the grounds, they could get to work." Her hand found his and squeezed. The gesture brought him more comfort than her words. "What I do know is they wouldn't let her go without a fight."

Winnie shifted suddenly and both of her little hands dropped on top of theirs, as if she was determined not to miss out on the hand hug. Delaney's laugh was awkward enough for both of them. Bruce could feel her trying to gently slip away but Winnie was having none of it.

"I didn't know you were awake," he said.

"Are you hungry?" Delaney asked. "If your dad says it's okay, I put chocolate treats in the bag."

Both female hands fled from his palm like the parting of the Red Sea. "Chocolate?" Winnie eyed him with a comically shocked face.

"I'm going to need some of that myself, as well as one of the sandwich wraps," Delaney said. "I suggest we all eat our fill. We don't have much time. We're almost there."

There, meaning the mysterious quiet place. If only *quiet* meant the same thing as *safe*.

NINE

The bus pulled up to a stop and the door opened. This time, Delaney took the lead down the bus aisle, searching through the windows. No other vehicles were anywhere near the bus stop. Given that school wasn't in session, the college campus was relatively empty.

Bruce, with Winnie's little hand in his, joined her on the sidewalk. "Are we heading to another safe house?"

"No. I believe Marshal Bradford wants to meet us at a spot with little foot traffic inside Reiman Gardens."

Bruce silently processed the information. "Reiman Gardens? Why didn't you say so? Winnie loves it there. It's a smart meeting place, really. It's seventeen acres of fully enclosed beauty with good security. I don't remember any cameras or anything that could be hacked."

She wanted to be relieved, but if the past twenty-four hours were any indication, she couldn't allow her guard to inch down, even for a second.

It only took a couple of minutes to enter the front door to the main building where cold air-conditioning blasted them. There was no line to pay admission to the volunteers stationed at the desk. They passed a sign that read, Iowa Police Chief Association Leadership

Lecture Series. Hunziker House. Delaney glanced at the map of the gardens. The meeting place was too big of a coincidence.

"Wow. So did your boss lead us to the safest place in town or what?"

Delaney wouldn't go that far, but she acknowledged the firepower and experience in one room would be considerable. "Maybe the entire state?"

He pointed at the top of the map. "I know where the conference room is. It's not a long walk." Bruce said.

"It's also not where I was told to go." She pointed to a trail on the map that veered through a couple of the gardens and ended up at a spot near the Prairie Vista. "We need to get here. We'll go off the path and wait at the benches that are supposed to be behind the trees."

Delaney pointed to the photographs in the hallway, hoping to divert Winnie's attention as they passed by the entrance to the enclosed butterfly exhibit. "Don't worry," Bruce said. "She only likes to look at them from afar. She hates bugs that have the audacity to land on her."

Slightly hesitant to leave the indoors, she pressed the door that led them outside. With a canvas of deep green, splashes of every color in the prism spread across the designed landscapes. They were passing by a small gardener's shed when Winnie shouted, "Gnomie!"

To her right, stairs led up to a statue of a bearded old man holding a yellow flower and wearing a red hat. The hat alone had to be at least five feet tall. All told, the statue must've been a good fifteen feet. The sign next to it read World's Largest Gnome. Someone had used white marker to insert *Concrete* as a modifier.

Bruce lifted Winnie into his arms as she tried to run up the stairs to see it. "His name is Elwood, but Winnie insists on calling him Gnomie. He'd actually be good to hide behind."

"I'll keep that in mind." Delaney made sure no one was around before she led them onto an unmarked path. A bench was right where Bradford had described. Surrounded by trees, no one would see them without intentionally going off the path. Winnie bent over and smelled some purple bell-shaped flowers next to a sign identifying it as Summer Peek-A-Boo Onion. They settled onto the bench, but Delaney kept her senses engaged with their surroundings.

"How do we go about getting into WITSEC?"

Delaney spun to face Bruce. "I thought you said that you would do everything you could to avoid that." An unfamiliar heaviness settled on her chest at the thought of him leaving for good.

"That was before seeing Nanc—" His throat choked with emotion. A rustling of leaves sounded next to the small pond. Delaney sprang upright and stepped in front of Bruce and Winnie, placing her hand on her gun before she even thought about it.

"It's Bradford," the gruff voice said before he stepped out. Admiration shone from his eyes. "I knew you'd figure out what I was talking about. I remember telling you how much I love this place."

"I'm assuming you typically use the normal paths to get here." She clicked her holster closed once more.

"Yes, but I felt the need to take extra precautions." He glanced at his watch. "I've only got a few minutes."

"I have to say I'm a little surprised you're still a member of the police chief's association."

"Oh, I'm not anymore. I'm the featured speaker." He winked and knelt down to smile at Winnie. He presented her with a bendable stick that had a butterfly loosely attached, as if flying. "If your dad says it's okay for you to keep it, I bought you a toy from the gift shop."

Winnie grabbed it and let it flutter in the breeze, flashing him a smile bright enough to light the shaded area by itself.

Bruce's frown didn't let up, though. "You look familiar. Have we met?"

The words tickled Delaney's ears. He'd said the same thing to her at their first meeting, but in her case, it'd been true. Apparently they'd met during college, though she still found it hard to believe she couldn't remember him. Granted, it had been before she'd really worked at honing her facial recognition skills.

"I get told that a lot. Take a seat." Marshal Bradford pointed to the bench. Delaney couldn't help but feel a little unsettled that the marshal had changed the topic without directly answering Bruce's question.

"Do you have news about Mrs. King?"

Bradford's shoulders sank and Delaney's stomach turned hard as rock, preparing for the worst. "She survived the shooting, and we have every reason to believe she'll make a full recovery."

Bruce's breath escaped him, and he rocked forward with his eyes closed. "Thank God."

Delaney sent a silent prayer of thanks as well, but Bradford's demeanor still set her on edge. "And the deputy?"

"He's in ICU, but we're hoping for the same prognosis."

Then why wasn't the marshal looking and sounding more positive while he delivered the news? Bradford's lips formed a straight line. "Nancy King is no longer a witness."

"What?" She hoped she'd misunderstood.

"She refused any further protection. She booked a flight to her daughter's in Wisconsin. Says she's ready to retire and be a full-time grandma."

Bruce's face fell.

"I'm sorry," she said.

Bruce shook his head and shrugged. "I knew she would be getting ready for retirement soon anyway, but I didn't want to think about it." He seemed to take great interest in the leaves swaying in the trees. "I'm just sorry Winnie and I didn't get a chance to say goodbye."

Delaney's heart hurt for him. It was hard to find people to trust. "I'm sure when the trial is over, she would be happy for you to contact her." That is, if he didn't end up in WITSEC.

Bruce turned to Marshal Bradford. "What if I videotape my testimony? What if Nancy did? She might consider that, if you asked. Could we skip trying to get me to the courthouse? And—" he glanced at Delaney "—if things don't get better, when do we start talking about WITSEC?"

"When we think the danger won't end at trial, we'll discuss your enrollment in the program. Right now, the assistant attorney still believes your testimony has the power to turn Mr. Andy Bowers into the informant we need to bring down the organization. If that happens, we will no longer need your testimony. But I can't make guarantees. We take your safety seriously, Mr. Walker, and I will be the first to recommend witness protection if it becomes necessary."

Bradford checked his watch. "As far as video testimony goes, that option has already been turned down. We always suggest that alternative before the Marshals get involved. Unfortunately, the US Attorney's Office is determined to ensure the witnesses have face-to-face time with the jury. It's much easier for a jury to trust a witness if they can see your expressions and tone of voice without a recording desensitizing the experience. Not to sound flippant, but in their trial experience, the witness with the best story wins the jury over."

He turned to Delaney. "Which is part of the reason I'm here. After the incident this morning, the judge has expedited the trial. We have two weeks to get the witness safely to the courthouse or he's releasing Mr. Bowers from prison."

"Still no murder weapon?"

"No. It would make our lives abundantly easier if we could find it. So, for now, I want to encourage you that we're doing all we can on our end. Keep your chin up, and this will all be over soon." Marshal Bradford stood. "Deputy Marshal Patton, may I have a word?"

They stepped to the side of the path, just out of earshot of Bruce. "Are we worried about a mole in the Marshals?" Delaney asked before Bradford had a chance to speak.

Bradford's eyes widened for a split second before he put his hands on his waist. "I would be foolish if I said it was impossible, but I can't imagine that's the case. The more likely scenario is we have a weak security link in our communication. So I want you to go silent." He handed her a pager. "If it's necessary to reach you, I'll page you with a number to call me. It's my understanding there are still a few Casey's General Stores that have pay phones."

"Sir, I don't think it's wise to return to the same—"

"No, of course not." He handed her a slip of paper with a handwritten address. "Do you know where this is?"

The address was on one of the county gravel roads most people never traversed, but the name caught her off guard. "You're sending us to a prairie?"

"Funded by a government grant. It's not an official safe house yet, but some law enforcement officials live on the land. They'll be expecting you."

"Who else knows about this place and has this address?"

"You and me. That's it."

"Sir." Delaney glanced over her shoulder. "Given all that's gone wrong, I wonder if another deputy would be more quali—"

Bradford grinned as if he'd known all along she would try to bow out. "You're the perfect deputy for this assignment. I insist you remain the lead on this. Trust me."

If any other man in the world had said those last two words to her, Delaney would've instantly done the opposite. No one could be ordered to trust. Trust had to be earned. But in Bradford's case, he'd already earned hers. His confidence in her boosted her morale. She memorized the address and handed it back to him to destroy. "We better get moving, then. You have a vehicle for me?"

"Yes." He handed her a set of Chevy keys. "Brown rusted thing. Third row, closest to the building. Car seat already installed. Two other marshals are waiting at opposite ends of the parking lot. They'll escort you to the county line, but then they have orders to turn around. You'll only be a mile or so away by then anyway."

The fact they still didn't know how the CryptTakers kept finding them nagged at her. "Fine. I welcome a caravan. I'd like to ask for a couple of days at this safe house before there's any further attempt at communication from the US Attorney's Office. If we can be at the safe house for two days without an attack, then I'll be more apt to believe we don't have a mole within our ranks."

He glanced at his watch. "Fair enough. The decision isn't up to me, but I'll make the suggestion. I've got to go." In a much softer voice, he added, "Stay safe."

The flowers and trees had produced a calming effect on Bruce, even though he wouldn't fully unclench his stomach. Winnie knew the gardens well enough that she grew restless with wandering around just one secluded area. She wanted to wave at Gnomie again, make music with the dancing wind chimes and run through the maze. But the way Delaney tilted her head toward the parking lot after she came back from her talk with the marshal made it clear that it was time for them to leave.

"She seems comfortable here. You said you've been here a lot?" Delaney asked as she made her own path through the grass.

"Yes." Winnie was happy to match his stride and keep up with Delaney without a word. "Being out in nature always reminds me that despite my good intentions, when I don't have control, God does. So this was good timing."

She smiled in response but the smile faded when they stopped in front of a brown car covered with rust spots. Two minutes later, they were on the road. The Chevy had no bells or whistles, but at least it had air-conditioning, though the smell coming out of the vents rivaled some of his dirty socks after a long run.

A walkie-talkie sat in the middle of the front seat, and

a bag of water bottles sat on the floorboards, but otherwise there was no sign that the car had been left by the Marshals. Delaney glanced in the mirrors. "I'm not going to use any communications unless absolutely necessary."

"Can I ask where we're going?"

"Basically the middle of nowhere. Except it should be a wonderful place for Winnie. If it's in the location that I'm picturing, you both will have the space to stretch your legs and run."

"For how long?"

"A few days at the most. The next time we leave, we'll visit the courthouse. It will be a one-day affair where the attorneys will do the pretrial interviews early in the morning, followed by your testimony later that day."

Delaney drove through Ames with their escorts a couple cars behind until she came to a two-lane highway and turned north. The stretch of highway had no other cars and, given the flat stretch of land, it seemed to never end. The radio crackled. "Mix it up."

One of the deputies passed them to take the lead.

"Do they know where we're going?"

"No. When they see the county line, they have orders to turn around, which will happen in just a few minutes."

The cornfields on either side of the highway waved their husks at them. In the distance, wind turbines turned. The slow revolution of the blades somehow calmed him, slowing down the pace of his own breathing. Just past the fields and wind farm, a thick layer of forest completed the view.

"Moo cow," Winnie shouted.

To the right a wooden-fenced area held cows grazing in front of a red ranch house. It passed in a blur as Delaney sped up.

Bruce glanced at the speedometer. They'd left the fifty-five-mile-an-hour speed limit in the dust. "Is something wrong?"

"Probably not. I imagine the other deputies are in as big a hurry as I am to get to the safe house. The deputy in the Jeep behind me keeps speeding up."

Bruce stretched his arm backward and gave Winnie's knee a small squeeze as he looked over his shoulder, out the back window. A small object appeared on the horizon, following the Jeep. Bruce flinched, hoping he was seeing things.

He leaned forward and studied the side mirror. A black object in the air darted from the highway to pass over the cornfields, sailing over the crops at the same speed as their vehicle. "I think I know why the Jeep is speeding up."

The radio crackled again. "Are you guys seeing what I'm seeing?"

"It's a drone," Bruce told Delaney. The thing looked like a miniature helicopter, though he couldn't get a very good look at it, given the flying object was roughly a hundred feet away.

Delaney turned to face him. "A drone?" She took a look for herself, her knuckles turning white as she gripped the steering wheel. She grabbed the radio. "Affirmative. Drone. Over." She let the static fill the air. "There's no procedure for how to handle this. I'd really like one hour where I didn't have to get creative."

"It's not necessarily something to be afraid of. It could be an agricultural drone. They're really taking up a huge part of the commercial drone market right now."

"What are farms doing with drones?"

"Fertilizing, spraying insecticide, examining the crops."

The object zoomed to the left, hovering over the cornfields as if demonstrating that Bruce could be right.

"Yeah, well, until we have some kind of confirmation that we're dealing with a tech-savvy farmer we need to assume the worst."

Bruce kept an eye on the drone's path and his neck tingled with discomfort. "I don't think agricultural drones usually keep up with cars going sixty miles an hour."

Delaney pursed her lips. "Do you know if drones that size can be weaponized?"

"Maybe. I'm not really close enough to see the size of the thing." Bruce unbuckled his seat belt.

"What do you think you're doing?"

Bruce dived through the small space between the two front seats.

"If you kick me, we're going to have more problems than that drone," Delaney snapped.

Winnie laughed at her dad's awkward positions as he tried to scoot next to her in the back seat. "There's no way I'm letting Winnie be exposed to the windows." He would throw his body over her car seat, if need be, before he'd let the drone target her.

On the floor, a long US Marshals bag peeked out from underneath the driver's seat. Bruce leaned over and tugged on it. "I didn't notice this before. It looks like they equipped the car with a gear bag for you."

"Yes, I know. It should all be standard-issue. See what's inside, please."

The radio buzzed. "Possible unfriendlies approaching from the gravel road to the west. Over."

Bruce squinted and leaned forward. About a mile

north, a black truck with men in the back sped toward the highway, dust clouds billowing behind it. He spun around to look out the back window. Behind the Jeep another black truck was approaching quickly. "It's an ambush." The words fell from his mouth as his heart pounded fast against his ribs.

Delaney's gun appeared in her right hand while her left hand stayed on the wheel.

Bruce unzipped the gear bag and felt momentarily paralyzed by the amount of firepower in front of him. He'd never used a gun before, other than to shoot at cans at a homemade firing range as teenager, but he would do anything to keep Winnie safe.

"I need you to buckle up," Delaney said before he could pull a weapon out of the bag. "We're about to go off-roading."

She didn't give him a chance to even consider following the suggestion. The car spun in a sharp right and lurched as it crashed through rows of corn, filling his ears with the sound of leaves slapping against the car. Delaney swerved and they bounced over a ridge of dirt before the wheels found the path that a tractor most likely used between the sections of farmland.

"Sorry. Didn't go as smoothly as I wanted."

Probably because she didn't brake at all before taking the turn at full speed. The other deputies couldn't be seen anymore. Corn taller than the car was on either side. "You didn't radio them."

"No. My responsibility is getting you to safety."

The car's engine grew louder in volume. She had to be pushing the pedal to the floorboard. Every couple of seconds, Bruce's torso lurched forward and almost hit the seat in front of him. Neither the dirt road nor their vehicle was made for high speeds.

Rapid cracks sounded in the distance. Bruce held his breath and prayed silently that the deputy marshals on the highway stayed safe.

"I'm sure they're better shots than the guys in the trucks," Delaney said. Bruce wasn't sure if she was trying to convince him or herself. "Let's hope they got the drone," she continued. "I'm pretty confident that thing wasn't in the air to check on the corn."

He'd already arrived at the same conclusion. Roughly a quarter mile ahead, the wind turbines they'd seen from the road spun at the same lazy pace. Where the sight had calmed him before, somehow it irritated him now that they weren't spinning faster, as if they were supposed to match his mood.

They closed the distance and Bruce marveled at the enormity of the machines. He hadn't realized just how big they were before. At almost three hundred feet in height, each blade looked to be the same size as a wing from a 747.

Delaney groaned.

Bruce looked through each of the windows but didn't see what had caused that reaction. "What? What is it?"

"The good news is I don't see any manned vehicles following us. The bad news is I see two unmanned." Delaney veered a sharp right to avoid a particularly deep rut. "Do you know how to load a shotgun?"

TEN

Delaney wondered what Marshal Bradford would say about a potential mole now. Except Bradford said no one else knew the address. She wouldn't have even seen the drones if she hadn't hit a particularly large bump while looking in the side mirror. The smallest glimpse of something in the air led her to sink down in her seat and peek in the other mirror.

"I've almost got the gun loaded, but I don't think you're going to want to shoot so close to the wind turbines. Wha— Did you see that?"

She stiffened. "See what?"

"I thought for a second that the drone was going to run into the turbine, but instead, it expertly maneuvered around a turning blade."

"How could it do that, unless… Do you think the operator is close enough to have a visual?"

"Doubtful. These are long-range drones. More likely, it means that the drones have proximity sensors—sonar, radio, optical. Maybe even acoustic." He said it with a sort of reverence.

"So is that important for me to appreciate them before I shoot them down?"

Bruce was right that she couldn't even attempt to take the drones down when they hovered by the wind farm. The legality of shooting down the drones in the first place was problematic. She could legitimize the need underneath the protection of the witness, but the FAA was going to send piles of paperwork her way if news got back to them.

"It means it's not going to be easy," he said. "Designers have worked to make them harder to attack. Apparently, they'd already discovered that was going to be one of the big problems in transitioning to drone delivery for retailers. If I'm right, these drones will have been programmed to use the sensors for evasive maneuvers."

"Well, that's just great news." She wasn't a sniper by any means, but she had spent an abundance of time on the firing range. She'd never had flying targets that were programmed with defensive measures, though.

"If only I had my computer. If I couldn't bring them down, we could at least find out the origin of their commands."

She understood the sentiment, even though it wasn't very practical at the moment. Being able to use the drones to track the operators was a very interesting idea, though. Could she disable the thing without destroying it? She couldn't imagine something built so small for speed and maneuverability having the bulk to be able to handle the discharge of a weapon, but Delaney couldn't risk being wrong.

No more cracks of guns from the highway could be heard. They'd traveled far enough into the fields that they were completely isolated. That didn't mean that more gunmen weren't on the way, especially with the drones still following, tracking their speed down the dirt road. Maybe the cameras weren't able to see inside the car yet. They'd left the wind turbines in the dust.

Up another quarter of a mile was a grove of trees. If she wanted to try to take the drones down, now was the time.

"I'm going for it." She slammed on the brakes and spun the wheel slightly to park diagonally across the road. Bruce shoved the shotgun through the space over the console. "You'll have a better chance with this." In return, she handed him her handgun. "Stay down."

She unlocked the car door, pumped the shotgun and kicked the door open in order to keep both hands on the weapon. The drone directly in front of her must have recognized the weapon because it ascended rapidly in the air, like a model rocket. So Bruce was right. The drones had been programmed with evasive maneuvers. She aimed and took a shot. The drone veered to the left but wobbled in the air. Some of the pellets had to have hit the rotors.

She lifted the gun to aim once more. The drone soared to the right this time but wobbled, as if it was laughing at her. She didn't wait for it to regain balance and shot again. It shattered in the air, plastic pieces raining over the field.

So much for merely disabling it. She pumped the next shell and turned to aim at the other drone. Except she couldn't find it anywhere. It had disappeared. Bruce tapped the back window. "It's hiding in the corn."

"You must be kidding." Well, if it was hiding, maybe they could get out of sight before it reappeared. The car was still running when she hopped back into the driver's seat and aimed the nose at the grove of trees.

"You played tag with the toy?" Winnie asked.

Delaney glanced in the mirror. Bruce's shoulders almost reached his ears. "I didn't know how else to explain."

If there hadn't been people trying to kill them, she would've found the description adorable. It served as a good reminder that keeping Winnie calm and happy would go a long way to keeping them safe. She remembered the way Bruce had gotten Winnie to cooperate with hiding and being quiet back at the hotel. "Since Winnie likes to play hide-and-seek, I think we should stop and do that because I don't think I'm going to be able to keep driving the car once we reach the trees."

"Hide?" Winnie asked.

"Yes, except I think we're going to hide with you," Bruce said.

"No, I want Laney to find me."

Laney? No one had ever called her that, except for a frat boy who tried to boss her into going out with him. He hadn't made the same mistake twice. *Laney* didn't sound like a hard-hitting law enforcement officer. Neither did Delaney, but at least it had a more official-sounding ring to it. Hearing the nickname said sweetly by a toddler, though, was something she wouldn't mind hearing again.

Bruce didn't acknowledge Winnie's request. "Are you going to radio the other marshals to come get us?"

That was actually the last thing she had in mind. Could she trust anyone? For all she knew the Crypt-Takers had gotten to someone on the inside. Given their reputation for contracted jobs with foreign powers, the organization likely had monetary resources that would make most government employees stumble. How else did the hackers keep finding their location?

"No. Not yet. We're going to the safe house alone."

"Alone? Do you really think that's a good idea? How will we defend ourselves if more trucks full of men show up in front and behind us? Even if I used this— this—well, I don't know what it's called but I'm willing to shoot it. I just don't know how good I'll be. But even if we were both armed, they would still outnumber us."

She needed to keep Bruce calm. Logic flew out the window when panic got its claws into witnesses. "I'm aware of the situation, Bruce, but right now I need to focus on getting that drone to stop watching us."

He leaned back in his seat and blew out a breath. "It popped up again. Hovering over the fields."

Delaney slowed down just enough to slip under the canopy of leaves and park. The strip of trees was roughly a hundred feet wide, split down the middle by a thin trickle of water at the bottom of a low, muddy bank. One large step and they would be able to cross. On the other side of the grove, another cornfield began.

"Take Winnie with you and hide in one of those rows. Don't run once you're there. Walk. Those leaves can slice you like paper cuts if you brush against them at high speeds."

He unbuckled Winnie's car seat and disappeared past a grouping of old birch and red elm trees. She made a mental note of exactly where they hid so she didn't aim anywhere in their direction. Delaney heard the hum of the drone's blades before she saw it.

This drone looked like a square with three fins sticking up in the back and two fins pointing down to the ground. The blades moved so fast they looked like blurry gray air. She stepped behind a thick trunk and waited, acclimating to the sounds of the small forest.

If it were true that the drone had acoustic sensors, she would have to be fast.

The high-pitched hum grew louder. Winnie's squeal reached her ears. If she had heard Winnie, then the drone might have, as well. Delaney rounded the corner and shouted, hoping the drone would be attracted to the loudest noise. It spun in place, a camera lens reflecting off the sun hovering over the horizon to the left.

She raised her weapon and shot. The drone zoomed to the right, not a hint of the wobbling that the other drone had exhibited. It was getting dangerously close to the edge of the forest. She couldn't shoot it now that it was in the line of Bruce and Win—

Bruce's head popped out of a row of corn. She wanted to shout out, to tell him to stay down, but that wouldn't help matters. Delaney ran for a tree ten feet in front of her, hoping to lead the drone away from her protectees. She looked over her shoulder. Bruce had picked up a branch that was at least three inches thick at the center and swung it over his shoulder. There was no way he'd be able to hit the drone—it was staying too high up for him to be able to reach. But the drone would easily be able to reach Bruce, especially if it had a small weapon on it. The only thing that made sense was for Delaney to distract the drone, overwhelm it with—the shotgun.

Delaney fired, shooting the shotgun shell high in the sky. Leaves and twigs exploded all around her. Bruce had let the branch in his hands go and it hurtled, flipping end over end directly toward her and the drone that was stuttering, unsure of which direction to go as the forest leaves rained down from the bullet's disruption.

Like a bat hitting a baseball out of the stadium, the

branch struck the drone right in the middle. The crack of metal and plastic breaking echoed underneath the trees. Delaney dropped to the ground as the drone soared over her head until it smacked into the trunk of a walnut tree.

Delaney didn't waste any time. It was still mostly intact and could take off at any moment. Or worse, transmit the data to the men with guns to show that it had found Bruce and Winnie.

Bruce's heart pounded against his chest. He'd seen the dark cylindrical thing hanging underneath the drone and didn't know if it was a camera or a weapon. The only thing he knew was a flying Frisbee was not taking out Delaney or his daughter. He rushed forward to help Delaney finish off the thing, but Delaney held up a finger over her mouth and stepped on the drone. She grabbed a nearby rock the size of a softball and smashed the remaining rotors that still spun, clearly attempting to get back in the air.

She flipped it over and after a few targeted hits, the black cylinder underneath snapped off. Why was she methodically taking it apart? She opened a panel and her eyes widened. She inserted her fingers and exhaled. "I think the power is completely off." She stood and carried the drone to the trunk of the car.

"I'm not sure turning off the power from the drone is enough to stop the tracking."

"Even if I unplugged the power? I was hoping the Marshals could use it to reverse track the origin."

"Might be safer to leave it at a landmark you could lead them to."

She set the machine against a tree. "True. You know more about drones than I do."

He wouldn't argue that point. Before the year of betrayal—he probably should stop thinking of it that way if he wanted to get over it—he had researched them thoroughly, tossing the idea around of investing in drones that would give lightshows, similar to fireworks. He wanted to give back to the community, and it sounded like a perfect gift. He hadn't given it a single thought in months. "Don't like them as much as I used to."

"Being chased by them can have that effect. Hey, how'd you take it down anyway? That was an impressive throw."

"You can thank my javelin throwing days in college. Muscle memory."

"Do I need to go find Winnie?"

"That's what she wants, yes." He'd never been so thankful that his daughter's favorite game was hide-and-seek. It made the countless times he'd had to "find" her behind their couch at home worth it. Maybe, after this was all done, she'd even be willing to hide in different locations.

Delaney crossed the space between them. She came to the row of corn and squatted. "Oh, where, oh, where is Winnie?"

A giggle sounded and Winnie dived into Delaney's chest.

Delaney lost her balance and fell backward, her arms encasing Winnie. His daughter's giggles were like a balm. Delaney's wide eyes met his before she closed them and a hearty, rich laugh escaped. Winnie giggled harder and slapped her little hands on Delaney's shoulders as she stood over Delaney.

"Need a hand?" He scooped Winnie up with his right

arm and offered his left to Delaney. She wiped away a few tears before she accepted and stood. The action seemed to remove all traces of humor.

A fire had returned to her eyes. "I think they must be tracking us. You owned an iPhone. You know the find feature that shows a map, a blue dot with a geographic circle estimating the location?"

"Of course. A GPS tracker."

"That's the only explanation I can figure on how those drones found our exact location."

Unnatural cold seeped into his bones. "What are you saying?"

Her eyes narrowed. "I'm saying they might be tracking you specifically. Maybe you have something on your person. If you do, we'll never get free. Another truck, another drone… We can never escape if you don't fess up."

Bruce pulled his chin back. Was she insinuating that he was hiding a phone and endangering them on purpose? "You can search me right now."

It might've been his imagination or the breeze that blew underneath the trees, but her cheeks seemed to redden. She tilted her head. "If you didn't bring any electronics, then we need to check all your clothes. I don't know how, but maybe they planted something on you."

"Almost every item I have on was either given to me by you or your team."

She nodded. "If we've been compromised by someone on my team, then we better find out. It doesn't change that I need you to check every inch of your clothing. Don't forget your shoes. I'll check your bag." She strode to the car. "Maybe we can do it while we drive. We need to hurry, Bruce. Assume there are more of them on their way."

He strode to the vehicle and decided to sit in the back with Winnie again. "You're not planning to drive through the woods, are you?"

She picked up the shotgun from the ground and placed it, nose down, on the front floorboards next to the console. "I just need to get over the creek bed and there should be another access road in between those fields."

Bruce strapped Winnie into the car seat as Delaney dumped out the contents of the mailbag onto the front-passenger seat. Winnie kicked her feet and squirmed against Bruce. "Lovey!"

Delaney picked up the item in question and let the satin edge of the blanket slip through her fingers. She felt along all four edges before she smiled and handed it back. "Okay. Here you go."

Bruce hopped in the back as Delaney started the car and aimed between two elm trees.

Winnie pressed Lovey up against her cheek in a soothing motion. Something bothered him, but he wasn't sure what. He tried to ignore the lurches of the vehicle over rocks and logs. "Why…why did you feel her blanket that way? You don't think it's possible someone could've placed a tracker on her, do you? She's only worn her own clothes from home. Maybe we should stop and check the car seat the Marshals provided."

Delaney nodded. "Maybe. We need to be thorough."

He reached over and took the seam of Winnie's shirt between his forefinger and thumb. Winnie squirmed, with a laugh. "No tickle, Daddy."

Bruce tried to smile but his insides twisted. If the

CryptTakers had gotten to him, he could deal with that, but how would they have even had the opportunity to have gotten to his daughter? He removed her right shoe. She released a high-pitched angry scream. Delaney slammed on the brakes. "What? What happened?"

"She's mad at me. She doesn't understand why I'm taking her shoes off. One second, sweetie." The tread, aside from a little mud, didn't appear to have anything stuck to it. He felt along the inside seams and pressed along the sole. He froze.

The soles were plain white. The rainbow-colored shoe logo in the center had disappeared. It was possible it had worn off from use, though she'd only had the pair for two months. He reached over and removed the other shoe. This time Winnie frowned and watched him but didn't complain. Also no logo. Not even a faint outline or indention where it used to be.

"Hold on," Delaney said. "This seems like the most shallow part of the creek bed." The car bounced violently as she drove it on a diagonal. The back tires spun for half a second. She downshifted and made it over the other side where she sped up, but a sickening crack sounded as the car jolted over another bump. "I don't like the sound of that," Delaney said. "But it's still running so we're going to keep going with it."

The engine revved and she turned a sharp corner. The side mirror crashed against the line of cornstalks. A minute later, she found the access road and pulled onto it. Bruce hadn't realized he'd been holding his breath until she straightened and drove straight.

He returned his focus to Winnie's shoe. The sole was stiff but wasn't glued into the shoe like he'd thought. It slid out to cries of "No, Daddy! Don't break it."

"I'll fix it."

She sniffed. "You'll fix it?" Her little voice, full of trust and hope almost broke him. The sole definitely wasn't part of the original shoe.

"Did you find something?" Delaney asked.

"Maybe." He turned the foam to the side. It was two layers. He stuck his thumbnail into the seam and worked until it split apart just enough for him to fit his fingers in and pull. The glue gave way and the two parts divided. An electronic chip with an attached battery nested inside the bottom half of the sole. "Stop the car."

She braked without question. He barely made it out of the vehicle before his stomach lurched and gave up its contents.

"Are you okay? I think I can stay straight for a while."

He slowly straightened, his back still to the car. "It's not your driving. I found this." He held up the tracker, still attached to the broken sole. He sucked in a breath of fresh air and turned to meet her eyes. "They've been tracking my daughter all along."

ELEVEN

Delaney tried to make sense of what he was showing her. "It was in her shoe?"

"Yes." He extracted the tracker, then shook the flimsy thing in the air and reared back his arm as if to throw it.

"No. Stop!"

"I don't want it near her."

"I know that and I agree. But it's better to lead them far away from her instead of close." She pointed down the road. In a few feet, the land sloped down, leading to a set of railroad tracks.

She thought she'd heard the sound of a far-off horn a moment ago. Just then, the distinctive horn blasted again. "Do you hear it? Get in. Find something to tie the soles together and let's get the tracker on that train."

Bruce's face fell. "I think we have another problem." He pointed to the dirt behind the car. A long, black line went straight back to the grove of trees they'd exited. "Looks like we're leaking oil."

No, no, no. She really needed something to go right. Every second they spent in the outdoors was another moment another drone or gunmen could appear. "Are you a mechanic?"

"I wouldn't say that, no. I know enough to get by."

"Then let's hope the damage isn't serious. Get in." She didn't wait for him to fully close the car door before she stepped on the gas pedal. The telltale chugging sound grew closer. "It better be a long train because it's fast approaching."

The car pitched forward and stopped responding to the pedal. Cloudy billows of smoke or steam poured from under the hood. At this rate, they were going to miss the train. "Do you have the shoes ready?"

"Let me do this. I need to do this. Get Winnie out for me, please." Bruce jumped from the car and with what looked like a US Marshals shirt tied around the two soles he'd removed, he sprinted past the white puffs still slipping out of the car.

Delaney gritted her teeth. He hadn't even taken a weapon with him. She pulled Winnie out of the car seat and watched him run down the dirt road.

"Daddy's fast."

"Yes, he is." She'd forgotten Bruce was a runner, but obviously his legs remembered. The man knew how to race, and his long legs took him at a speed she could only match for maybe a minute. He, however, showed no signs of stopping. At least she knew he was good at throwing.

Winnie grabbed her face with both hands. "Let's run. Catch him."

For half a second Delaney wanted to do just that. But the entire reason Bruce ran was to keep his little girl safe. He was trusting her with Winnie. Now more than ever, she needed to be cautious. Delaney scanned the area. So far no hints of anyone else coming, but that could change in a heartbeat.

The thunderous roar of the train could be felt and heard before she saw it rushing past the fields at the bottom of the hill. The freight train's rust-colored containers were almost a blur. Clearly there was no intersection to cross anytime soon. The train traveled at a faster speed than she'd seen before.

Winnie held her hands over her ears. "Too loud."

Bruce picked up something off the ground—maybe a rock to add weight—and put the object inside one of the shirtsleeves, which he tied together in a knot. He pulled his arm back and the blue shirt soared into the air.

The shirt bounced off the roof of one of the containers. Her entire body tensed. It wasn't going to work.

The shirt seemed to blow in the breeze as it spun to the next container and began to fall to the ground. At the last second, it jerked, caught by what appeared to be a ladder on the back of the final container. Delaney hadn't realized she'd been holding her breath until she exhaled.

The shirt remained fully attached to the train as it sped away. Bruce turned and jogged back up the hill toward them, as the blue-and-yellow-striped caboose took the loud sound of metal drumming against metal away with it.

"I want my shoes on."

Delaney glanced at Winnie's socks. "Let's see what we can do." Bruce had left them discarded on the floorboards. She feared they would be bumpy and utterly uncomfortable with the inner sole removed, but it looked as if the thin original soles had been left underneath the fake ones.

She set Winnie down on the driver's-side seat, perpendicular to the steering wheel, and bent over to put on the shoes before helping her stand upright on the road. "Is that better?" Winnie's grin was all the answer she needed.

She looked up to find Bruce staring at her as if he'd never seen her before. She touched her face self-consciously and ran her fingers through her ponytail just in case she had twigs or leaves attached in odd places. More likely, he was still upset that someone had been tracking Winnie. For that matter, she was upset about it herself. "I'll want your help in making a list of everyone who had contact with her from the moment you went to work Saturday morning until now. I'll cross-reference it myself to make sure each person is investigated until we find out who did it."

He blinked rapidly. "I'll take a quick look at the car, but I think it's a lost cause." He leaned forward and for the briefest of moments Delaney wondered if he was going to kiss her. "Excuse me." His voice was almost a whisper but all that registered were his gorgeous green eyes. He squinted in confusion before he twisted around her and pulled the hood-release valve.

She took a step back, finally understanding that had been his intention all along. Maybe the sun had addled her brain. "I'll take a look at the map. We need to get out of here as fast as possible."

He lifted the hood, sweat glistening on his forearms. "If I had to guess, we ran over something that broke the oil pan. No oil means a very hot engine so it blew the radiator and seized up."

She pulled out the Iowa map from the side door pocket. "I'm guessing you can't fix it."

A slow smile spread across his face. "Yeah, you could say that." He shut the hood and picked up Winnie, scanning the horizon.

Delaney put the weapons back in the black gun case, zipped it up and threw the handles over her right shoulder. She reloaded the mailbag with the snacks and water bottles and handed it to Bruce.

The walk wasn't going to be comfortable with a bag of firepower on her back, but she wasn't about to lead her charge into the plains without a way to protect them. At least the case was padded so the sharp edge of the shotgun wouldn't bother her. "I hate to say it, but I think we need to walk north through the cornfield for a while."

He frowned. "Can't we follow the train tracks instead?"

"But the train tracks offer heavy exposure and access. I want to be where we're least expected and with some cover if anything else decides to hover over us."

His shoulders dropped. "Understood. Come on, sweetie."

"We're going to walk in the plants?"

"At least for a little bit," Delaney answered, double-checking the map. "Hopefully not too long. Maybe a quarter of a mile."

Bruce stepped in between the rows of stalks. The tops of the leaves just passed his head. In another month or so, harvest season would begin. The stalks would reach almost twelve feet.

"This is making me hungry for corn on the cob," Bruce said.

"This is field corn. I'm pretty sure you wouldn't enjoy it as much as sweet corn."

Winnie ran around his legs and led the way down the path. Delaney didn't mind, seeing as Bruce's shoulders brushed against the leaves that tried to slap her if she got too close.

"How'd you know that running in corn rows would cut you? Do that a lot as a kid, did you?"

"I detasseled in the summer like almost every other teenager in my class. Have you never done it?"

He shook his head. "No. We moved around a fair amount when I was growing up. It's why I wanted to make sure I could build a stable life for Winnie, so she could make friends and feel like part of a community. So you grew up here?"

"Actually Southern Iowa, but I came here for a lot of events in high school and college and never left."

"What was it like growing up in one place? In Iowa?"

"Um, I don't know. The biggest excitement was football games and different festivals. At the time I thought I could never live long enough to grow up. It just seemed so endlessly far away."

"Like you were on an endless escalator where the view never changes?"

She laughed. "Yes. Like that. Only when you grow up and it finally does change, it isn't quite what you'd imagined."

Truth was, she'd had a great childhood. It was adulthood that had gone badly. The plan had never been to fall into an unhealthy relationship, ending up unwed and pregnant. Somewhere along that escalator, she got lost.

"I'm pretty sure every kid feels like that no matter where they grow up. At least, I did. Your parents must be excited to have you back in the Midwest."

Dread settled in her stomach. "Actually, I haven't told

them." What had gotten into her that she was revealing things that were none of his business? Her heart beat faster as she smacked the corn leaves out of her way. "Yet," she added. She would have to face her family sooner or later, but she didn't want to let Bruce know the reasons they were estranged in the first place. She shouldn't care what he thought.

She did care, though. His compassion and dedication to do the right thing were more attractive than his green eyes, his warm smile, his broad shoulders... She grimaced. He was proving just as dangerous to her heart as his daughter.

Despite the snapping and rustling of leaves, Bruce noticed the change in Delaney's tone. He'd hit on a sore spot, but he didn't know if she'd want to talk about it or if it was best to change the subject. He was a little emotionally drained himself, so he wasn't sure if he should risk a conversation that could be a potential minefield.

The rage over someone putting a tracker in his daughter's favorite shoes had fueled his frantic run to the train. The fire in his bones had continued to sizzle until he saw Delaney bent down, helping his daughter with her shoes.

Then the anger fizzled, giving way to a warm liquid feeling as if he'd just put on his favorite sweatshirt and drunk a cup of warm cocoa. The waves in Delaney's ponytail had blown backward as she smiled at Winnie. His girls only had eyes for each—

Bruce stumbled over a rock in the dirt but caught himself before falling over Winnie. His girls? Where had that come from? He blew out a breath. Until he knew for sure whether he would have to take Winnie into WITSEC, he needed a better rein on his heart. Besides, it was probably just a logical longing for a family again. That was all.

"Okay, fine, you win." Delaney huffed. "Your silence is deafening. I can almost hear the questions spinning in your brain."

He nearly laughed. Thankfully, she couldn't really hear his thoughts or she'd be horrified. "I wasn't sure if you wanted to talk about it."

"I don't, but I know how persistent you can be." She took a deep breath. "My family is disappointed in me. I made a series of decisions a few years ago—ones I very much regret now—but when they made their feelings known at the time I couldn't really handle hearing them. So I shut them out."

"Does it by chance have to do with Raymond?" The question was out before he could filter it.

"Yes. But you probably know more than you ever wanted to know about your assigned deputy now."

He stopped and turned so he could look at her wide blue eyes. "I don't think of you as my assigned deputy. I'd like to think that if we'd met at a different time, in a different situation, we could've been..." He knew he'd said too much when she stepped backward, her lip slightly curled as if horrified. "Friends. I hope that doesn't offend you."

Her shoulders sagged in what looked like relief. "Uh, no." She tilted her head and looked past him. "Winnie didn't slow down. We should keep up with her."

He should've kept his big mouth closed.

Winnie still pumped her arms, purposeful and strong, clearly enjoying the feeling of being in charge, leading adults down the row. A burst of light roughly twenty feet ahead promised open spaces. The stalks suddenly leaned to the right, smacking Bruce in the forehead. He rushed forward to hold his arms over his daughter's head in case they got too close to her. "Do you know what the forecast is today?"

"No, but it is August in Iowa. Anything can happen."

As if agreeing with her, a rumble in the distance sounded.

"We should be fine," she added, though she didn't sound convinced. "A storm should significantly decrease the chance of drones discovering us. Let me go ahead of you two and check the road."

He turned sideways and she tried to step past him but they ended up face-to-face. Her breath still smelled like the peanut-butter chocolate she ate on the bus. "I didn't peg you for a silver lining type of person." He met her eyes but couldn't stop his gaze from drifting to her lips.

She sucked in a breath, visibly flustered by their close proximity. "I must be spending too much time with you." A smile played on the edges of her lips as she moved past him and Winnie. "You're a runner, right? If my map is current, we have roughly a mile due east before a little-known road will take us right to the safe house. I think we can walk again once we get past the railroad tracks, as there'll be a fair amount of tree cover. Think you can run that far while she piggybacks?"

"Maybe not piggyback. I don't think her legs can wrap around my back, but she's light enough I can hold her with one arm." He needed to at least be able to pump one arm if he was going to run fast. His right thigh twinged at the thought of it.

While Bruce ran often, he didn't often sprint like he had done to get the tracker onto the freight train. He'd strained one muscle but it wasn't so bad he couldn't work through the pain. The gear bag on Delaney's back looked heavy, probably a good twenty pounds. "You sure you can run with that?"

She turned back and rolled her eyes. "I wouldn't have brought it up if I couldn't do it. Marshal basic training academy taught me a lot, but what I remember most is the running." She sighed. "So much running."

She held one hand up as an indicator to stay back as she stuck her head out of the row of corn and pulled it back in. "Wait," she whispered.

For a second the only noises were crickets in the distance and stalks brushing against each other from the wind. A low rumbling of large motors grew in volume accompanied by snapping branches. Delaney swung the bag around her torso so the front rested on her chest as she unzipped the bag and slipped her hand inside.

Bruce picked up Winnie. There was no chance he was going to let her run ahead and risk getting caught in the crossfire. The rumbling sound faded as fast as it had crescendoed. Sweat dripped down his neck.

Winnie wrinkled her nose. "You're wet, Daddy."

"I know, sweetie."

"Stay put." Delaney stuck her head out a second time before she disappeared entirely. Seconds turned into minutes, and for a brief moment, Bruce wondered if she'd given up on them. "Come out," she called.

Bruce had changed his mind. Corn was the last thing he craved, although butter and salt on anything sounded good. His stomach growled.

Delaney had zipped her gun bag up. "They went down the other tractor road and sped off after the train.

By now, they've passed the curve and won't be able to see us."

"Same trucks as before?"

Delaney paled. "Not sure, but we can't take any chances."

Did her reaction mean the deputy marshals they'd left behind on the main highway hadn't survived? Delaney shook her head as if thinking the same thing. "For all we know, these men got away and circled back around. I think it's safe to say getting the trackers on the train worked."

For some reason, that didn't soothe Bruce's nerves. "I'm ready."

"Stay on the opposite side of the dirt road from me. If you hear anything, see anything out of place, or I point at you, hide in the fields. I'll cover you." She patted the strap of her bag. "Run hard until we get under the cover of the trees then we'll catch a breath and reevaluate." She eyed Winnie and broke out a smile that would've fried a wattage meter. "Remember when you said you wanted to run together? Let's go." Delaney took off at a run without another word.

"Catch her, Daddy!" Winnie's words prompted him into motion but his mind and heart were trying to catch up with his limbs. If they hadn't been running for their lives, would he have been bothered by Winnie's enthusiasm, as if they were on a family run? She giggled as she bounced in his arms, the noise jarring his senses. As if to heighten every emotion on purpose, the heavens erupted with rain. His feet slid slightly as the dirt turned to slick mud within seconds.

He squinted, and as Delaney swung her arms in rhythm, he thought he detected the smallest of smiles.

"Are you enjoying this?" he shouted over the rain. Winnie's hair hung down the sides of her face, providing the illusion that her blue eyes had doubled in size. She giggled again when Delaney flashed another smile.

"The only spot we're fully out in the open is when we cross the railroad tracks. With this rain, there's no way they can see us."

The tightness across his chest didn't let up. Delaney probably didn't understand that the high-tech drones that had been following them could fly and see just fine in rain or snow. He just hoped he had a chance to tell her before they were spotted.

TWELVE

The horrible weather was fitting. The moment the skies had erupted, Delaney fought the urge to cry, scream and yell, but it was so perfectly in keeping with this whole assignment that she had to laugh. Everything that could've gone wrong about the case, had, and she wasn't going to let a little—okay, a lot—of rain be her breaking point. She would make sure Bruce and Winnie got to safety if it was the last thing she did. Though she really didn't want it to be the last thing.

Keeping up with Bruce's long stride was slightly challenging, but she managed. They both leaped over the train tracks and didn't slow down until the rain decreased to a drizzle underneath the trees. Delaney stopped underneath a thick oak's covering and wrung out her ponytail.

"Do that to me," Winnie said, eyes ever watchful. Delaney didn't hesitate and leaned over to squeeze the moisture from her hair. Winnie's smile and the intensity of Bruce's gaze heated her chest despite the raindrops chilling her arms.

Did Delaney's daughter have a mother and father who right now were laughing in the rain together? Or were they watching the rain from inside as they prepared dinner together?

She didn't want to look directly at Bruce, but she couldn't help it. She was drawn to him. Was this what had happened to Kurt with his witness Rebecca?

Sudden clarity caused her to step backward. "Kurt."

Bruce frowned, confused. "Your mentor?"

"Yes." She gestured with her head for him to start walking north under cover of the branches. "If I got to a pay phone, say at a gas station, could I call him without worrying about someone tracking us."

He shrugged. "The CryptTakers would have no reason to be monitoring a pay phone or Kurt. You said he's in Idaho?" She nodded. "You might be onto something. You could use him as a middleman to get us some help."

"We're almost to the safe house. If I remember right, there is an old mom-and-pop gas station just half a mile from here." They continued walking in silence and Delaney wondered if he had picked up on her thoughts about family. If so, it had likely scared him even more than it scared her. She was falling for Bruce, and she couldn't let her heart soften any more. It couldn't survive breaking a second time.

She didn't deserve a family, and he would never understand why she had given up her daughter. A wave of sorrow, so unexpected, took her breath away.

"Are you okay? Did you twist your ankle or something?"

Delaney swallowed and kept her eyes focused on the leaves. "I'm fine. Sorry." The hardness around her heart had been softening for days, leaving her vulnerable in a way she hadn't been in years. She needed her guard back. Now.

"Daddy, I don't want to be wet anymore."

It was just the focus she needed. "Then let's get you somewhere dry." Thankfully, aside from the tops of their heads and shoulders, they weren't drenched, and the strong warm wind blowing from the west helped fight the effects of humidity as well as sending the large rain cloud past them so that by the time they stepped out of the trees there was barely a drizzle.

She'd never been so thankful to wear shorts on the job, as it helped her walk quickly without discomfort. Her senses heightened as they found the gravel county road and crossed the intersection. It only took a few more minutes to find the gas station, and by then the rain had ceased.

Fortunately the pay phone was located near the back. She couldn't recall if she'd ever called someone collect before, but she didn't have enough change to do otherwise. Since when did payphones charge fifty cents per call? Fortunately, Kurt's was one of the few numbers she had memorized. When the prompt asked her for her name she said instead, "I went to Iowa," to avoid using her name on the phone, just in case.

The phone clicked and she heard Kurt's voice accepting the charge. "I really want to tease you about calling collect, but I imagine this is serious."

"You imagine right. I'm calling from a pay phone because we're dealing with some heavy-duty techies that can track anyone."

Bruce's groan reached her ears, but she wasn't going to worry about proper titles like hackers or crackers. "I need you and Mike to do some undercover internal affairs." She listed the names of the deputies and police officers who'd had contact with Winnie between the murder of the security guard and Reiman Gardens. Kurt thought their IT guy, Mike, had the capability to find out if the law enforcement officers she'd mentioned had been in touch with the CryptTakers. "It isn't exactly procedure, but we can investigate their communications and accounts."

"It's a good thing we have leeway to do what we need to do, then."

"Uh-oh. You're starting to sound like me."

"I need to know if we have a mole." She swallowed hard. "And take a look at Marshal Bradford."

Kurt breathed out. "You once told me you would trust that man with your life."

It hurt to hear it aloud. "At the moment, I still do, but I need to know my trust isn't misguided." The sound of crunching gravel prompted her to end the call.

She stepped out of the booth and hid around the corner, where Bruce held a now-sleeping Winnie against his shoulder. Delaney sneaked a glance and watched a slow-moving red-and-white Ford pickup truck. The driver, wearing a red ball cap, looked over his shoulder briefly at the gas station. Delaney pulled her head back in, bumping up against Bruce's shoulder. "You need to stay back." She noticed Bruce's face had gone white. "What is it?"

"For a second I thought for sure that was my stepbrother."

Exhaustion must have fried Bruce's brain. "But it couldn't have been him."

Delaney led him behind a barn situated next to the gas station. "Your stepbrother? His name is Trevor, right? Why couldn't it have been him?"

Bruce laughed. "Because Trevor wouldn't be caught dead in an old junker, let alone wearing an old ball cap."

"You're saying he's fond of money, then."

A defensive streak he didn't know he still had flamed to life. "Who isn't? He likes nice things more than some of us. Always did."

They crept behind a shed until they reached a barbed wire fence. Delaney pointed due east and they remained on the small dirt trail next to the boundary. "You said Trevor is supposed to be in the Caribbean?"

"That's where he told me he was heading. Planned to sell all his possessions and move there to live it up after I bought him out."

"There should be a road over there that will lead us directly to the safe house." She adjusted her holster, not even trying to hide the handgun that she'd moved to her hip. "I need to make sure no one sees us approaching it."

The silence after the storm felt thick as he breathed in the air smelling of freshly cut grass.

"I know this is a sensitive topic, but—"

"You want to know how much I paid him." He'd been thinking about it, as well. "A million dollars."

She sputtered. "A million?"

"I don't have that kind of cash, if that's what you're wondering. I give myself a modest salary and any profit from the business goes back into investing in the company. We did have the assets in the company to pay Trevor, though. There was the potential for him to have made significantly more if he had just stayed. We had the ear of some big banking chains. I was actually supposed to meet with them Monday. Of course, now the entire company might go under, thanks to the Crypt-Takers."

"I want to promise you that your business is safe but—"

"I'm not asking you to, Delaney."

"A million dollars in the Caribbean could go fast. They've been hit hard with hurricanes in the past few years."

"I know, but I would like to think he would've contacted me if he got short on funds. I'd take him back in a heartbeat." Trevor's departure, especially after Shannon left, had cut him deeply, but he still felt that same compulsion to take care of him if Trevor needed help. Besides, they had once made a great team.

"You haven't had any contact with him since he left?"

She was touching on a sore spot and he didn't have enough energy to filter his words. "He was the one who left. I'd hoped he would've been the one to call me first." It sounded so petty when he heard himself say it aloud, but the feelings behind it were true. "I did try to call once, but he must have changed his cell number."

Delaney frowned and Bruce realized that made Trevor sound all the more suspicious. "Feel free to check him out, but I don't think he would have anything to do with this. He may be selfish, but he wouldn't ever try to kill me."

"Is your mother still married to his dad?"

"No. Quite frankly, Trevor's dad was a lowlife. I never liked him. After Trevor's dad ran off, who knows where, I suppose I felt a little overprotective. I may have only been a year older, but I've always watched out for him. Started in junior high and never stopped. Well, until recently. But it was his decision to leave."

They turned onto the side road she indicated. She kept glancing at him until he laughed. "You clearly want to ask something. Go ahead."

Her cheeks flushed. "Does she—" her head bob indicated Winnie "—know she's adopted?"

Bruce didn't know how Winnie was fast asleep in damp clothes in his arms, but he didn't blame her for being tired. She'd been a trouper. "The short answer is yes. Shannon actually wanted it that way."

"When you divorced?"

"Before, really. I think she was trying to prepare me and Winnie, in a small way." He sighed. "Shannon just wanted more in life."

"Sounds a little like your stepbrother."

He felt his eyebrows rise. "They were two peas in a pod in many ways. They were both in my ethical hacking group, and for a while I thought she was more into Trevor than me, though she insisted that wasn't the case."

Delaney looked pained by the news but didn't say anything.

"I think all along Shannon knew she might not stick around. She was already disappointed I had chosen to start the business in the Silicon Prairie instead of Silicon Valley. She wanted more excitement, and I wanted a family, so she thought a baby would provide both. When Winnie had health issues, Shannon couldn't cope."

Delaney stumbled and regained her balance. "Health issues?"

"Her vitals seemed normal when we first adopted her, but it turned out she had a heart defect. Her breathing was pretty fast. They called it patent ductus something or other. I could never say the diagnosis right. It basically meant that a heart vessel that should've closed after birth still diverted blood away from her lungs. They ended up shrinking it with medicine."

He could still remember putting his hand over her little body and pleading with God to help them find answers. "She didn't have to go through surgery, and after that her health was normal, but for the first month we were in the hospital a lot. Winnie was put on a ventilator and poked and prodded by specialists before they figured out what was going on." He'd never been so thankful as the day they'd left the hospital with a good prognosis. "Anyway, I think it's part of the reason Shannon never really bonded with Winnie, though how a mother could ever give up her child I'll never understand."

Tears gathered in Delaney's eyes and her body shuddered. "I had no idea Winnie... You went through all of that. Th-that had to be so hard."

Bruce wanted to pull Delaney into his arms. Her compassion overwhelmed his already full heart. He smiled. "Why would you? I doubt that's the sort of thing the Marshals would put in my file." He shifted Winnie slightly. "She's one tough cookie, a fighter. I think that's why she's done so well this week."

Delaney nodded and kept her eyes on the road, but he could tell she was still overcome with emotion. It was such a stark contrast to the all-business deputy he had met days ago, hard and determined to prove herself. Was this her true self? Soft and warm and full of love?

They passed a sign about a government-funded prairie. "How much farther?"

She stopped at a dirt driveway. "We're here."

"A prairie? No offense, but when someone is after me I prefer hard walls over camping underneath the stars."

"Don't worry. I've been assured the walls will be tough and filled with two law enforcement officials who hopefully are as averse to technology as my grand-parents." They passed the waist-high grasses and lavender until they spotted a stately house in the distance.

"You can't see that at all from the road," Bruce said. "I'd never have suspected a government-funded prairie would have a house on the land."

She picked up her pace. "Exactly. Let's hope they have some hot water and beds ready for us."

They climbed onto the stately porch, and Delaney knocked on the door. A petite lady with sharp eyes answered, then gaped.

Delaney's face had turned ashen. "Grandma?"

THIRTEEN

Her grandmother put her hand over her mouth, her fingers visibly shaking, before she reached out and pulled Delaney into her arms. "I've missed you so much, sweetheart." Delaney felt a kiss on her forehead before Grandma hollered, "Bob, come here!"

Delaney pressed her hand on her ear, still ringing from the shout at such a close distance. Out of the corner of her eye she could see Bruce fighting a laugh as Winnie stirred in his arms.

Grandma stepped back. "Come in, come in. I'm sorry. I got so excited to see my sweet pea I completely forgot to be quiet."

Winnie lifted her head, blinked slowly and studied Delaney's grandmother without saying a word. Grandma sucked in a deep breath. "She—she looks so much like you." Her eyes glistened as she turned back to Delaney. "You didn't put her up for adoption after all?"

If the floor opened up and swallowed her whole, Delaney would have welcomed it. Her stomach heated, and she kept her gaze on Grandma. "This is Bruce's daughter."

"Oh...oh." Grandma put a hand up in the air. "Of

course. I'm sorry. Same coloring of hair and eyes, I just thought…"

Delaney could feel Bruce's questions in the air, but she refused to look. Grandpa strode over the wooden floors, a frown firmly in place—probably because he hated when Grandma shouted for him—until his eyes widened at the sight of Delaney.

She was struck mute even as her grandpa's burly arms pulled her into a hug so fierce that she feared her nose would break against his chest. Grandpa was in his seventies now, and even though it'd been more than three years since she'd seen him, he could still be considered a bruiser.

He had retired as the chief of police in Waterloo years ago, where she'd thought they still lived. "Since when do you guys live on a prairie?"

Grandma gave Grandpa a glance. "Well, we figured out we both wanted to try homesteading. We took some classes, bought ourselves some property, built the house and applied for a grant. Before we knew it, we'd joined the network of prairies. We accept visitors—even class field trips—during certain times of year for all sorts of things. Oh, you should see your grandpa pulling a tractor load of kids around the property. The prairies help the farmers on either side of us as well, with nutrient deficiency and runoff problems and—"

Grandpa cleared his throat. Grandma laughed and placed a hand on her chest. "Well, I get excited," she said. Her eyes grew sad. "I'm glad we finally get to share it with you."

Grandpa folded his arms over his chest and leaned back. "Are you here for a visit or are you on official business?"

Grandma shook her head. "Surely not."

Delaney sucked in a deep breath. "I was told you agreed to act as a safe house."

Grandpa hung his head. "He could've told us you were the one coming."

"Why wouldn't he tell us?" Grandma asked.

Bradford knew good and well who her grandparents were. He also knew that Delaney had been estranged from her family ever since Raymond came into her life. Her parents and grandparents had never liked Raymond, despite the fact he was a fellow law enforcement officer.

Delaney shouldn't have trusted Bradford after all. Her anger could fester later, though, because at least his sneaky reconciliation skills proved to her that Bradford was definitely not the mole. He was still going to get an earful from her...later. He never mentioned the two law enforcement officials they'd be staying with would be retired and *related* to her.

Grandma shook her head and stared at the little girl. "I imagine this little one wants some cookies and dry clothes." Winnie wiggled out of Bruce's arms and accepted the hand Grandma offered.

Grandpa laughed at Bruce's face expression. "Don't you worry. We'll make sure she gets a healthy meal, too." He winked. "Or were you hoping to get a cookie, too?" Grandpa left the entryway, following Winnie and Grandma.

"I'm sorry. I had no idea it would be them," she said.

"Your grandparents were both in law enforcement?"

She exhaled, so thankful that was his first question. He must hate her right now, after Grandma had basically admitted she'd given up a child for adoption. Bruce had said it himself—*how could a mother ever give up her child?* He'd said he'd never understand. "Grandma worked as liaison with the public and Grandpa was a police chief. They met on the force."

He stared at her for a long moment, then nodded. "Your grandpa is right. I don't want to miss out on the cookies either." He walked after them, leaving her alone in the entryway. Framed photographs on the wall showed her mom and dad standing in front of the prairie sign.

"You've missed a lot." Her grandma's voice was soft and quiet behind her.

Delaney turned, but she didn't meet Grandma's eyes. "I wasn't welcome." Her voice cracked despite her best intentions.

"Excuse me?" Grandma pulled her chin back into her chest, surprise lining her features.

"Don't get me wrong, Grandma. I'm not proud of the decisions I made. I know I need to earn everyone's forgiveness. If I could go back and change—"

Grandma stepped forward shaking her head. "If you don't hear anything else, hear this. You always have been and always will be *welcome* wherever we are." She wrapped her fingers around Delaney's shoulders. "Sweetie, I don't know what exactly you remember, but we didn't shut you out. It was the other way around."

Delaney looked up at the light fixtures, reliving the heated conversations. "But you and Grandpa, my parents—"

"We didn't care for Raymond. We felt he didn't respect your dreams and... Well, we don't need to get into the particulars again. It's true we didn't like some of your life choices. I'm sure we could have communicated that in a more loving way, but, honey, we were only upset because we wanted the best for you. I know I can speak for your parents, as well. The last thing we wanted was to push you away. We wanted you to be happy!" She released a heavy sigh and stepped even closer. "We all tried to reach out after we heard about Raymond and the baby, but you had already moved, changed your number…" Grandma teared up. "It was obvious you didn't want to hear from us, but know that I hated not being there for you when you had to be in pain."

"I'm sorry, Grandma. I—"

"Sweetie, you don't need to apologize. We all have regrets on what we would've done differently. Maybe the one you really need to ask for forgiveness is—"

"I've already prayed, Grandma." Delaney's faith in her childhood years was largely due to her grandmother. Looking back, though, Delaney didn't really make it her own until she needed Him most.

Grandma smiled. "Good. Sometimes, though, even though we have God's forgiveness, we need to forgive ourselves before we can move on." She pulled Delaney into a hug. "Just remember we didn't deserve Christ dying for our sins either, so why can you accept His forgiveness but not forgive yourself?" She let her go. "I'm going to make sure your rooms are ready. Your grandpa is picking some corn for dinner."

Her words hovered in the thick air, and not just because Delaney dreaded the smell of corn at the moment. Had she really misinterpreted her family's concern? Isolated herself for years for no reason?

She hadn't meant to cause her family pain, but they had already been estranged before Raymond died. Delaney wouldn't have been able to handle the disappointed looks on their faces after they found out she'd given up her baby for adoption—she could barely cope as it was—which was why she'd left. Even now, there were traces of disappointment, but her softened heart couldn't battle it.

Was Grandma right? Did it hurt so much because she hadn't forgiven herself?

Bruce drank a cup of tea in the study, relishing the quiet and solitude, sitting in a leather easy chair surrounded by wooden shelves filled with encyclopedias and photo albums. One book, marked *Delaney*, caught his eye. He hesitated. Would it be a violation of her privacy? Though he supposed if they didn't want people looking through the albums, they wouldn't have displayed them on the shelves. He slipped the album out.

The photos were grainy and slightly faded, coming from a time when film was still processed. He skimmed the first few pages quickly. Aside from Winnie, he could never tell the difference between babies. The toddler photos, however, gave him pause. Delaney had the same color hair as Winnie, but the photos featured her in a police officer costume, standing proudly next to her parents. Her wide-eyed grin also reminded him of Winnie, but he supposed that was a trait all excited little girls shared.

He heard Delaney's groan before he noticed her in the room.

"I guess I'm busted," he said.

Delaney rolled her eyes. "I don't even know what all is in there. Let me save you before you reach the awkward teenage years."

He doubted she'd ever looked awkward, but he

handed the album over. "Is Winnie still keeping your grandma busy? Should I go give her a break? I feel bad she's still awake."

"We've completely messed up her sleeping schedule, haven't we?" Delaney sat down on the couch next to him. "Don't feel bad about Grandma. She's having the time of her life reading Winnie stories she hasn't pulled out in years. Before you know it, Winnie will be ready to go to sleep again." She glanced at him. "How are you holding up?"

"Fine."

She nodded. "Okay. Now for real."

He chuckled. "Well, if I don't think much about the last few days, I do better. If I let my mind go there, I wrestle with what I should've done differently."

"I respect that. You work so hard to do everything right." She fingered the corners of the album cover but didn't open it. "Once I got my life back on the right track with God, I worked hard to trust Him in most areas of my life but obviously failed in others, as evident by not getting in touch with family until now."

She released a sad laugh. "And I can't exactly say that I connected with them today by choice. If I had cared more in my early years about doing things the right way, maybe I wouldn't have let my feelings dictate so many of my decisions."

Bruce wasn't sure he always operated on logic. Sometimes he justified decisions with flimsy logic when really the choice was just what he wanted, but he wasn't ready to admit it aloud. "Did your time away from family have something to do with what your grandma said about adoption?"

Delaney's shoulders sagged. "I don't expect you to understand."

Except he wanted to know everything about her, even if it was hard to hear. Was she holding back the reason she'd been so aloof with Winnie at first? "I'd like to try."

She hung her head. "My fiancé—well, boyfriend, really, since he hadn't proposed officially—was Raymond, the cop I told you about." She stared up at the popcorn ceiling. "He pursued me like no one ever had while I was in my senior year of college. When he was accepted into the police academy after graduation, he said I should join him. I didn't want to risk losing him, so I did."

"You didn't want to go straight to the academy?"

She flipped open the album nonchalantly, letting her fingers drift over the protected photographs. "No. I wanted to go into forensics." Her eyes lit up just saying the word. "They analyze crime happening in the area and can use the data to predict when and where a crime might happen next. It's a fascinating field that's growing by leaps and bounds."

"But you didn't think Raymond would wait for you if you stayed in school for more training."

She nodded. "Before I knew it, years had gone by and I was still working on patrol. We worked opposite shifts most of the time, so we didn't even spend much time together. Living together seemed like it made sense— it made it easier to see each other, at least a little, even when our schedules didn't match up. It wasn't planned, but we got pregnant." She averted her eyes again. "When Raymond was killed, I was in my third trimester. The labor pains came out of the blue, and before I knew it, I was in the hospital—C-section—but it'd only been hours since Raymond's passing and I...I couldn't process or think clearly. All I knew was this baby deserved a mom and a dad who both desperately wanted..."

Her voice had dropped to a whisper, shaking with emotion. "I didn't feel mentally, emotionally or financially equipped to be a parent alone, and my shame kept me from asking my family for help."

She flipped blindly through more pages of the album. Her posture had stiffened and the aloof deputy who had originally come to his door returned. "I called Harvey Jeppsen when they wheeled me into the hospital room, alone. He said he knew the perfect couple. So I asked for a closed adoption." She cleared her throat. "I kissed her, and the nurses took her away."

"Her?" His stomach churned, unsettled for a brief moment.

She nodded. "I left the hospital and went straight to Raymond's funeral. I didn't tell anyone what I'd done except Marshal Bradford, because he was the one that had delivered the news about Raymond."

"He was the police chief then?"

"Yes. He drove me to the hospital. Anyway, I came home and knew something was wrong. I ended up back in emergency surgery because of a rare complication—a uterine hemorrhage. They wanted me to stay overnight for observation, and there was a pastor there, visiting some members of his congregation. A nurse sent him to talk to me."

Delaney smiled softly. "He didn't take the pain away, but he listened and talking helped clear my head. I'd started having doubts about the adoption, but it was too late to change anything." She shook her head. "Too many days had passed. So I decided then and there to get my life right, throw myself into my work, become someone my daughter could be proud of—"

Her voice cracked again and she flipped through the photo album pages more rapidly. "And someday, when she turns eighteen, and the adoption file is unsealed, I can find her." She let out a giant breath.

He leaned back into the couch, overwhelmed with emotion. "Thank you for telling me."

"So, now you know my entire story. I don't blame you if your opinion of me has changed. You said yourself you could never understand—"

He placed a hand over hers, resting on the album page. "My opinion of you hasn't changed. If anything, my admiration of you has only grown. I hate the situation you were in—feeling like you were on your own with no one to help you carry the load. But I understand the guilt and shame when you try so hard to do the right thing and it's not enough."

She glanced at his hand and looked up. "But you said you could never understand a mother giving up—"

It was as if she'd punched him in the stomach. "I meant in my ex-wife's situation, Delaney. I regret my words sounding like a blanket statement. I never meant to imply there aren't good reasons…" His throat constricted. He had so much more to say on the matter, but his muddled thoughts weren't cooperating. "I was extremely thankful for the chance to adopt Winnie. I'll never feel anything other than gratitude toward her birth mother. I don't think less of you."

"Really?" Her eyes, brimming with tears, were warm and inviting.

He leaned forward, unable to break the connection. "Really." He glanced down at her lips. She smiled and closed the distance between them. As their lips were about to touch—

"Daddy, look!" Thunderous footsteps ran across the threshold into the room. Bruce straightened, his heart pounding, and he pulled his hand away from Delaney's. If his daughter noticed their close proximity, she didn't indicate as much. Winnie had on a frilly pink dress. Her hair, barely dry after the bath Bruce had given her, curled around her face, and her blue eyes sparkled.

Delaney's grandma followed Winnie into the den. "Can you believe I still had your old Easter dress? I loved it too much to ever part with it."

Delaney gasped as her hand slid down the photo album. The action caught his eye, and he couldn't look away. Where her hand had once been, he now saw a photograph of a young Delaney wearing the same frilly pink dress. The girl in that picture and Winnie could've been sisters.

Delaney turned to him, her lips curled in horror. "I can't avoid it anymore. I need to ask you a question. When is Winnie's birthday?"

FOURTEEN

Grandma looked as confused as Bruce until she glanced down at the photo album in Delaney's lap. "Oh, my." Grandma straightened. "Come on, Winnie. I think I remember where I saved some toys."

"Toys?" Winnie ran after Grandma.

"Uh…her birthday is in October." Bruce's eyes held uncertainty.

"Was she born the night of the fifth?"

Bruce's chin dropped as he stared at the photograph and raised his head slowly. "Why do I get the idea you already know?" His eyes hardened. "Are you trying to say Winnie is yours?"

"I don't know, but I can't deny the nagging feelings. Still, it could all be coincidences."

His forehead creased and he stared at her, silent. He placed his hands on his knees, stood and paced across the floor, anger evident in his stride. Of course he'd be angry.

"I'm sorry. You don't have to tell me. It was a closed adoption. I know I don't have any right to know."

He blew out a breath and his features softened. He didn't look at her while he spoke. "The night of October fifth Harvey Jeppsen called me. He said there was a mom who, after a tragedy…" Understanding dawned on his face and he turned to look at her. "She wanted two good parents to adopt her child. He knew we were on a long waiting list for a baby, and he said we could avoid the wait if we got down to the hospital right away, though he couldn't serve as our lawyer since he was representing the birth mother."

Delaney's eyes burned as she fought the waves of emotion pouring over her. Winnie really was hers. Her little baby had been born with a heart defect and had suffered during the first month of her life. And Delaney hadn't been there for her. Delaney hung her head as an inner heat seared her cheeks and stomach.

"When did you know?" Bruce's voice shook.

"I didn't. I had suspicions. But for every hint that seemed to point in that direction, something else counterbalanced it." She closed the photo album in front of her and set it to the side. "When Harvey called my phone to speak to you, I was surprised to learn about that connection. He was my lawyer, but you said you didn't use him for the adoption. Her…her middle name is Olivia. I was initially going to name her that."

"Harvey told me the birth mom loved the name. It's why we kept it as her middle name."

She shook her head. "I'd convinced myself you just picked the name for the fun initials. You said I looked familiar and Winnie has my coloring, but when she was a newborn she had darker hair and darker eyes."

"Eye and hair color often change from when they're a newborn."

"I didn't know. I just had a nagging—"

"And you didn't share your suspicions with me? Were you just trying to get close to me to get close to her?"

She reared back as if she'd been slapped. She might as well have been for the pain his insinuation caused. "No, of course not."

"I thought we were... Well, never mind what I thought."

Delaney really wanted him to finish that sentence. What *had* he thought?

"Did you know when you were assigned to the case?" His words were clipped with a hard edge.

"No. I told you—I had no idea. I promise. All I knew going in was that you were a single father with full custody."

He shook his head, put his hands in his pockets and resumed pacing. "You had all these clues and yet you didn't say anything. What am I supposed to think?"

She closed her eyes so the tears wouldn't win as she spoke. "I didn't say anything because I couldn't admit she could be my daughter. I thought I would have to wait fifteen more years to meet her. I couldn't imagine it could be true because I didn't deserve for it to be true!"

The words came out in a flood before she could filter them. Grandma was right. She hadn't forgiven herself. Why was it that she could she let God forgive her but was unwilling to believe He could allow Delaney to meet her daughter earlier? And that her dad could be a man she was falling in lo—

Her eyes widened and she stopped the trail of thought right in its tracks. There was no point in thinking that way when Bruce would never want to see her again.

Delaney stood up to join him. "I stand by what I said earlier. You don't need to worry that I'll interfere in her life. I know I signed all my rights away." She would have to move out of Iowa. How could she know where Winnie lived without being close to her? It hit her all at once. Those times she'd held Winnie, she'd been holding her own daughter. If only she'd known in those moments, she wouldn't have held back her heart, she would've opened up the gates and savored every second. "I'm—I'm not asking to be a part, I know it's a closed—"

"Would you stop saying that? Of course you'll see her. You're her mother. I'm not a monster."

"I never said you were. In fact, you're the opposite. I couldn't have dreamed of a better father—"

"I wasn't the one who asked for the closed adoption!" It was as if he hadn't heard a word she'd just said. He looked up at the ceiling. "I…I need some time to process this."

"Yes." So did she. But how was she going to do that when both of them were in the same house? Could she even keep it a secret? She couldn't lie to them, and Grandma had already seen the photograph. She could just imagine how her grandparents were going to take the news.

"I won't ask you to keep this from them." Bruce gestured toward the doorway. "It's written all over your face."

Most people thought her face never revealed anything. In fact, she'd been told she had a blank resting face, but Bruce always saw more. Not that he would ever want anything to do with her after the case.

The doorbell rang. Delaney's hand moved to her holster. It was cruel that she had to be on the job right now, but with this new revelation she had all the more reason to make sure Bruce and Winnie stayed safe. "Stay here."

Grandpa appeared in the kitchen, his hand also resting suspiciously on his waist, ready for anything. "Sylvia, honey," he called out to Grandma. "Are we expecting anyone?"

Grandma exited the hallway with Winnie on her hip and her other hand on her waist. It didn't surprise Delaney that everyone was packing. The legacy of law enforcement in her family ran deep.

Grandma's curious eyes met Delaney's for the briefest of moments, but she didn't ask any questions. "No, I don't know of anyone coming over. I can't imagine a threat ringing the doorbell, though."

Grandpa kept his eye on the back door. "You never know. I've seen lots of diversion tactics. Better safe…"

"Okay, then." Grandma pointed at Bruce. "I think it'd be best if you came with me." Bruce took Winnie from her arms. Grandpa kept his head up as he bent down and opened a cupboard where he flipped open the floorboard, revealing a well-lit set of stairs.

Delaney's mouth dropped. "Have something to tell me, Grandpa?" Unless there were some active threats against her grandfather that she didn't know about, why did they need a secret basement?

He shrugged as he closed the door over them. "It's a tornado shelter." His expression looked sheepish. "It might double as a bomb shelter or panic room, with a fully stocked pantry, kitchen, living room and storage area. So we can be comfortable if we need to stay there."

"Of course it doubles as that." The sarcasm ran thick. She pointed. "You get the front. I'll guard the rear." Delaney situated herself so her back was against the fridge. Her vantage point afforded her a view of the windows, the back door and a sliver of the front door in the entryway.

Grandpa frowned. "Shipping truck is driving away. Package left on our front doorstep."

A bomb? Delaney ran past him onto the porch, her gun ready. There were actually two items on the porch. The first was a thin envelope addressed to her grandpa and stamped Same Day. She picked it up and felt every nook and cranny of the letter. It was too thin and flat to hold anything but a piece of paper. The return address was in Des Moines, but one she didn't recognize. The sender was listed. Kathy Bradford. Why would the marshal's wife send something? She eyed the second package suspiciously as she opened the letter.

Deputy Patton,
Threats against the Assistant US Attorney have been made. Package contains burner phones. Please call me. Didn't occur to me you might think package was a bomb until Kathy went to mail for me to avoid suspicion. (Hi, honey. It's Kathy. Miss seeing your face. We need to have you over for dinner once you get settled.)
Marshal Stephen Bradford (scribed by Kathy.)

If Delaney hadn't been emotionally exhausted, Kathy's note would've made her smile. Marshal Bradford would've never said *please* either, when issuing a direct order. She picked up the package and closed the door behind her. "All clear. It's from Bradford."

Grandpa moved to open the floorboard. "False alarm."

"Time to go back upstairs." Bruce's voice could be heard when the door opened.

Winnie complained, "But Grandma said we could use flashlights."

Ten minutes ago Delaney would've found it cute that the little girl was so comfortable calling a woman she'd just met Grandma. Now, knowing Winnie was her daughter, her heart beat so fast she felt dizzy. Delaney grabbed the top of the dining room chair to steady herself.

She didn't miss the way Grandpa gave her a sidelong glance. "I'm fine," she said softly. What did Bruce think of Winnie's innocent use of the name Grandma? Winnie didn't know the truth yet, so she'd probably just picked up on Delaney addressing her as such.

She didn't wait to see Bruce's expression. Their feet could be heard on the stairs, so she stepped back into the study and closed the door behind her as she pulled out the first burner phone. Before she called Bradford she wanted to see what Kurt had discovered. It took three rings before Kurt picked up. "It's Delaney. I'll only be using this number once."

"I wondered when you'd be checking in. You're not going to like what I found."

Bruce avoided meeting Sylvia's and Bob's eyes, but he could feel them both staring at him.

Mrs. Patton cleared her throat. "You can call me Sylvia, honey."

"I like Grandma." Winnie frowned, upset she was being asked to change.

It was just like Winnie to want to call her by the first name she'd heard Delaney say when they arrived.

She was stubborn that way, and had gotten attached to Delaney so quickly, seeming to want to copy her in every way.

Sylvia bit her lip, clearly unsure of what to say next. "It's okay," Bruce said. While he wasn't ready to tell Winnie that Delaney was her mom, she would know soon enough. It struck him that these people, the ones he'd instantly liked moments ago, were now, in a strange way, family. He couldn't process that.

"Time for bed." He scooped Winnie up in his arms and kissed the top of her head. As he went through their normal routine of songs and cuddles before pulling the covers up in the twin bed she'd proclaimed to be hers, every heart stopping moment in the study replayed on a loop. He had almost kissed Delaney. He'd felt so close to her before the bomb dropped.

At Winnie's request, he sat on the edge of the bed as she fell asleep. He wanted to believe Delaney when she said that she hadn't been trying to get close to him to get to Winnie, but he'd been betrayed badly before. Words were cheap.

He consoled himself with the thought that Delaney couldn't take Winnie away, but what was he to do with this new twist? He wouldn't want to deny Winnie the chance to get to know her mother. How was he going to cross that potential minefield? And, if he did believe Delaney, did that mean there was a possibility of a future together for the two of them?

Did his heart even matter in the equation? He let his chin drop to his chest. *I have no idea what the right thing to do is. I need help.*

A small vibration below his feet caused him to turn toward the doorway where Delaney stood. Her face had taken on that hard exterior he recalled from their first meeting. She lifted a thumb over her shoulder.

Winnie breathed loudly and deeply, a sure sign she had finally fallen asleep for the night. He tiptoed into the hallway and met Delaney in the living room.

"The trial is tomorrow," she said softly.

"Tomorrow? I thought we'd have time to—" he'd almost said *process* "—recover." His eyes caught sight of two black flip phones on the dining room table that had been snapped into pieces. "You have more news?"

She nodded. "None of the deputies in our caravan today were killed. They were able to capture the armed men."

He leaned forward. "Does that mean the danger is gone?"

"Unfortunately, no. They were hired men. In fact, they were former contractors for the government—"

He groaned and shook his head. "I don't like where this is headed. They thought they were hired by the government to kill me?"

"At first, to simply show a presence."

"Like the time they drove by and shot at the SUV?"

"Exactly. But two days ago they received word to eliminate you and Nancy." She exhaled. "We think the sniper at the courthouse was part of their unit, but I don't have confirmation yet. All the digital sanctions they received did look very official. The FBI is sorting it out. The good news is they are off the street."

"It doesn't mean the CryptTakers can't hire someone else using the same phony credentials, though, does it?"

"That's part of the reason the trial was moved to tomorrow, so it's less likely another private group can be hired." She sighed. "The last bit of news is that I talked to Kurt, and his sources couldn't find any Crypt-Taker connections to any of the deputies or Bradford."

"That's good news."

She shook her head. "In this case, it's not, because I still don't know who planted the trackers in Winnie's shoes. Can I assume Winnie had more than one pair of shoes?"

"Yes, she has many."

"So, how did someone know which pair to put the trackers in?"

"Do we know they weren't placed in every pair?"

She nodded. "Kurt thought of that and asked a detective in the Ames PD to make a visit to your house. No other trackers." She stepped forward. "Can you think of anyone who would want to track your daughter?"

He sank down onto the couch. He didn't miss how she emphasized *your daughter*. She was trying to make peace. He looked up into her eyes. If he could do it all over again, when she'd first told him the news, he would've done everything differently.

It wasn't as if he'd never thought about meeting Winnie's birth mom. He just thought it'd be years down the road. He'd even researched the right things to say, but they'd all flown out of his head because it was Delaney. How could it be her? The woman he was falling in lo— No. He wouldn't even let himself think that way. He didn't want to be in another unequal relationship where the person didn't feel as strongly about him. He steeled his mind. "First off. She's your daughter, too."

A sharp breath from the other room snagged his attention. Well, if Sylvia wasn't sure before, she knew now.

Delaney blushed. "As soon as we get to the courts,

I'll make sure you're assigned different protection." She hung her head. "I won't deny that I want to be part of her life, but I accept the consequences of my decision those years ago. I won't push. You can take as much time as you need."

Her words sounded rehearsed, but they still squeezed his heart. Did she genuinely figure out Winnie was her daughter at the same time he did? He wanted to believe she'd been honest with him, but it was so hard to trust. He shoved away the thoughts and avoided commenting on her statement. He wasn't ready to make any decisions.

"As far as who would track her, I don't know anyone in my life that would do such a thing. The shoes... They were an early birthday gift from Trevor. Has her favorite character on them. Everyone that knew us would've noticed it was the only pair she would wear ever since she got them, even with dresses."

"Your stepbrother gave them to her?"

He nodded. "He said he didn't think he'd be back in the States in time for her birthday." Bruce didn't like the look on Delaney's face. "He may be selfish and a bit materialistic, but he's always loved Winnie. And I know for a fact that the trackers weren't in the soles that originally came with the shoes."

Her brow furrowed. "You said he was in your ethical hacking group from college?"

"Yes, but so were Shannon and a handful of other people I still consider friends. Most of them weren't great at it. It's a tough skill to master. They were mostly there to support the few of us who were better suited to it, and because our computer science professor promised extra credit if we learned."

Bruce ticked off the points on his fingers. "Shannon was great at coding but didn't have the knack for creating. She needed someone to tell her exactly what they wanted. On the other hand, Trevor is a jack-of-all-trades guy. He could do well at any of the parts of programming if he'd actually put his mind to it, but he wanted so much variety in his life he was much better at visioning and selling."

"All the same, I'm going to use another burner to see if we can get a location on Trevor. Especially since you thought you saw him."

"I'm telling you, it couldn't have been him." Although he didn't know why he was being defensive. It hurt that Trevor hadn't kept in touch. Maybe he needed to step back from his emotions in this and let Delaney take whatever steps the situation required. "But better safe than sorry," he conceded.

She gave him a pointed look. "You should get some sleep. Tomorrow is going to be a long day."

"You think it'll finally be over?"

She stilled. "It'll either be over or we'll know it's time for WITSEC." Her voice quavered on the last word. They wouldn't see each other again if he and Winnie went into the program. Unless she came with them. He wasn't going to say it, though. Not yet. He needed a week to clear his head, but all he was going to get was a night, so he prayed the Lord would work wonders with the time allotted.

Her grandparents walked into the living room. Sylvia wrung her hands, but it was the retired chief who spoke. "I know there's a lot of tension and things to sort in this room, but we want you to know we will respect your decisions."

Sylvia stepped forward. "Keep in mind that we would be happy to watch Winnie here while you're at court for the day. You've already seen we are armed and ready for anything."

Anything. The word filled with uncertainty was what he feared most.

FIFTEEN

Four in the morning didn't come as fast as Delaney would've liked. She tossed and turned for the few hours she had to sleep. Finally, she grabbed a cup of coffee and stiffened at the strange humming noises coming from outside.

"Don't worry. They're prairie chickens," Grandpa said. "They do the funniest dance, bouncing up and down trying to attract a mate, and it's always before the day's light. If you were able to stay longer, I'd make sure you got to see it. Bird-watchers come from all over to see them."

"You really love it here, don't you? The prairie life suits you as much as Grandma."

"Once you find something you love, you do what you have to in order to be near it."

Delaney almost rolled her eyes. It was obvious he wasn't talking about the prairie. "I want to arrive at the court before business hours, which means a 5:00 a.m. departure."

Grandpa agreed with her thinking. No one would expect them to arrive before sunrise. Every move she made today would need to be unpredictable.

Bruce must've employed the same strategy of thinking because he came into the living room and asked Grandpa if he could take up Sylvia's offer to watch Winnie. Grandma overheard and entered the living room, still in her quilted bathrobe. She nodded rapidly and accepted a mug of coffee from Grandpa. Grandma held up the mug but didn't drink, trying to cover up her giant smile. Delaney wasn't fooled, though, as she spotted the way her grandmother's eyes crinkled with joy.

Grandpa was already fully dressed in a flannel shirt and khaki pants—his preferred method for avoiding mosquitos—for his predawn walk around the perimeter of the prairie before breakfast. He didn't say anything about Bruce's decision either, but the way he beamed said it all.

As far as she knew, Winnie was their first great-grandchild, but Delaney couldn't bring herself to say that to Bruce. A fresh wave of shame washed over her at what could've been.

They got into Grandpa's truck but would only drive it for fifteen minutes. She pulled her shoulders back and focused on the country road ahead. They stopped at a storage unit where Grandpa kept old police souvenirs and an extra car he said they'd only used on long road trips to save gas.

Marshal Bradford had offered to send another caravan, but the way Delaney saw it, the more potential digital footprints accompanying them, the more risk of attack. They changed vehicles at the storage unit and got on the road again.

Silence had been her best friend for the past thirty-four months, but it betrayed her during the drive to Des Moines. Instead of soothing her and giving her the headspace to maintain a calm, logical outlook, the absence of Bruce's voice tensed her muscles. He sat in the seat next to her and perused the fields as the sun crested the horizon.

She stuck to back roads and avoided all highways and freeways. Miles of plains in either direction made her feel even more alone. The car was without a radio, so the minutes ticked by slowly. But eventually the sky grew brighter. On the final turn toward Des Moines, the phone she'd placed in the cup holder rattled. "I forgot to tell you that burner phone is yours."

He finally looked at her. "Oh?"

"I gave my grandparents a phone as well, with only that number programmed. If they have any questions or problems, they promised to call you. I also gave them another phone to call me in case you can't answer."

His eyes warmed, provoking her skin to flush. "Thank you."

Ten more minutes of torturous silence brought them to within a block of their destination.

"Delaney—"

"Yes?" She sounded too eager, too breathless. She leaned back in her seat and tried to sound more professional. "Is everything okay?"

His gaze went to her lips and back to her eyes. "Promise me you won't leave today. I know you said you'll resign from my detail, but before we part ways, I want to talk. No matter what happens in there, I want to…talk."

His tone held no hint of good or bad. What was he going to say? That he wanted her to stay away for the next fifteen years? Her throat closed at the thought, but if that was his decision then she'd respect it. At least she knew Winnie had a great father. A great father who deserved to find someone who loved him and would support him and…

"Okay. I'll make sure we find somewhere to talk before the end of the day." She blinked away the burning sensation in her eyes to finish the journey.

This time, they entered the gate without bullets. Deputies in plainclothes appeared from parked cars and surrounded Bruce when he stepped out. Delaney kept her eye on the skies, the moon barely visible as the sky lightened into a lovely shade of blue. The deputies formed a ring around Bruce until they climbed the steps and were safely within the courthouse.

A law clerk waited for Bruce on the other side of the security scanner. As they crossed over, Delaney couldn't help but feel she was crossing back over into a life without him. Flanked by other deputies, Bruce disappeared into the elevator, on his way to the pretrial interview.

"Good work. I knew you were the right one for the job."

Delaney spun around at Bradford's voice. She'd held back her fury when they'd spoke on the phone the previous night, waiting for this moment when she could express her feelings face-to-face, both for herself and her grandparents. "Did you know?"

Bradford's face broke into a wide smile. He registered the scowl she knew she wore and a shadow crept over his joyful demeanor. "No."

"You're a horrible liar." She stepped dangerously close to a line she would normally never think of crossing with a superior, someone who had the power to shut down her career forever. But he was more than a boss. Bradford was a friend, or so she'd thought, and the feeling of betrayal ran hot in her veins. "You *did* know. Otherwise you wouldn't know what I was talking about. You sent me to my grandparents, and don't even try to deny that you knew who they were."

"Oh, that. Yes, I did know about your grandparents."

"And you withheld the information from Bruce's background check that would've tipped me off to Winnie being my—my—" The anger bubbled up so hot in her throat that it choked off her words. She fought back tears and took sharp, jagged breaths to regain her composure.

Bradford stepped closer and placed a hand on her shoulder. "Now, that I didn't know about." He closed his eyes at the sound of her harrumph. "I *suspected*, nothing more. Her adoption papers were sealed so I had no way of knowing for sure. But when I saw Bruce's photo in the file…" He seemed to be at a loss for words. "I was in the hospital, in the waiting room, when you had your little girl."

She shook her head. "I thought you left after you dropped me off. I didn't see you later. Not until you came when I needed the emergency surgery days later."

"I also stayed there the night you gave birth. One of the nurses told me you decided to give up your baby for adoption. No one was there for you at the hospital. I knew you were estranged from your family and didn't know any other way to help except to be there in case you needed somebody to talk to. But when I came to check on you after the delivery, they had given you something so you could sleep."

Delaney couldn't hold on to her anger. Instead, tears of gratitude fought to get past her defenses. "I didn't know you were there."

Bradford looked up into the sky as if seeing the night

again in his mind. "I turned to leave and was walking down the hallway when a young man ran into the lobby, nervous and shaking with excitement. He held a car seat and had a diaper bag slung over his shoulder."

"You saw Bruce."

He nodded. "I saw Bruce. I didn't know his name at the time, but I hung out in the lobby for a little bit. I know I probably shouldn't have, but I wanted to know if your little girl was going to be in good hands. I knew you had a certain amount of time to legally change your mind."

"You were going to strong-arm me into keeping my daughter if Bruce rubbed you the wrong way?"

"I had every intention of doing what I thought was best for your baby, but this man loved her. The lady with him was much more subdued, but she seemed okay. Competent and gentle, at least."

Tears rushed down Delaney's cheeks. "I never should've let her go. I should've been stronger."

He put his hands on her cheeks and looked into her eyes. "You were doing the best you could with the information and resources you had."

She closed her eyes. "I couldn't even fathom ever being able to work again. I thought I was going to end up homeless and alone and couldn't do that to her. It took me weeks to realize that I would survive, one foot in front of another. I could have made a home for her, but it was too late by the time I realized I shouldn't have let her go."

He pulled her into a hug. Delaney stiffened at first, embarrassed that another deputy might see her hugging their boss, but then she decided she didn't care.

She stepped back. "Is that why you sent for me to

come back to Iowa? You thought I was ready to get her back?"

"No. I had no idea Bruce would become a witness. I kept an eye on your career and genuinely thought you would be a great addition to the team." He shrugged. "I might've been a little quicker to become involved in the case after I saw Bruce's photograph."

"To make sure I was lead?"

"As for your grandparents, I heard that they won a prairie grant and I always thought that would make a good safe house."

Delaney noticed he'd ignored her question, but she let it go. "And the perfect forced reconciliation situation?"

He shrugged.

"I suppose I should thank you." She sniffed and regained her composure.

"Does Bruce know that she's your..."

"Yes." The word came out as a whisper.

"Is he going to let you see her?"

"I...I don't know. I refuse to push the issue. Right now, I'm trying to be thankful that I got to see her at all—" Her throat tightened. "And she's so wonderful. And...and...he's such a wonderful father."

Bradford's left eyebrow raised. "You've fallen for him." He grinned again, and she had the irrational desire to slap it right off his face. "That's wonderful."

"No, it's not. It only complicates matters." She took a deep breath. "I plan to turn in my two weeks' notice at the end of the day."

His look of disappointment almost leveled her. "Delaney, don't be hasty."

She forced a sad smile. "You have good reason to say that, given my past, but this decision is actually the opposite. I've always known that I would step away from law enforcement if I ever got the chance to be with my daughter. I'm going to find a job in Ames. As safe and boring as possible."

"A desk job."

"Yes. Ideally with the department, but I'll take any job to be available in the event Bruce and Winnie need me."

"And if they don't?"

"Then I'll be content with being available and waiting." The phone on her belt vibrated. Delaney recognized the number. "It's my grandma's burner phone. She's watching Winnie today."

Delaney clicked the green answer button on the flip phone but didn't get a chance to speak.

"He took her. I don't know how he did it. It was as if he knew exactly where she was. One second she was running down the hallway and the next she was in his arms and he had a gun on her before we could—"

Her veins ran cold. "Who, Grandma? Who took her?"

"Your grandpa has an APB out. Everyone is looking."

"Who took her?" Delaney's voice grew so loud it echoed in the hallway.

"A man. He saw the two burner phones on the dining room table. I had labeled them so I wouldn't mix them up. He took the one labeled Bruce and disappeared with her."

The vibrating interrupted Bruce's train of thought as he relived Max's death in front of the attorney. He pulled the phone out of his pocket. It had to be about

Winnie. He'd forgotten to tell Sylvia that Winnie normally got a cup of milk before working up an appetite for breakfast.

He held up a hand. "Sorry. I have to get this."

The lawyer released an exasperated sigh. "Five-minute break."

He stepped out to the hallway and answered. "Hello?"

"Don't testify."

Bruce recognized the voice immediately. "Trevor? What's going on?"

"I'm doing my best to keep you and Winnie safe, but you keep getting in the way. I shouldn't even be talking to you, so listen. Don't mess with these people." Trevor overenunciated each word. "Leave the trial and go home. Let me fix things and you'll get Winnie back and your life will return to normal by tomorrow. Just trust me."

The words his stepbrother spewed weren't making sense. The slap of shoes against polished stone echoed throughout the hall, and he looked up to see Delaney sprinting around the corner toward him. Bruce squeezed the phone tighter. "What do you mean 'get Winnie back'?"

"She's safe with me as long as you go home right now. Don't say another word."

"Trevor!" His angry cry never reached his stepbrother as the call ended.

Delaney's eyes widened as she stopped right in front of him. "Trevor?"

Bruce lifted up his hand to throw the cell down the hall, but Delaney's hand cupped over his fist. "You might be able to call him back."

"Doubtful." He let her take the phone from his

hand, though. Rage pumped his heart so fast his vision blurred. How could Trevor betray him like this? They were family. Maybe not by blood, but it still counted for something, didn't it?

Trevor couldn't have sent those shoes for the purpose of tracking Winnie. He couldn't have known Andy would kill Max and leave Bruce as the only witness. But he knew Winnie would love the shoes so much that a tracker planted by someone else—someone Trevor told what to do—could be used to find Winnie and, by extension, Bruce. How could his brother do this to them?

"I can't be a witness." His voice croaked. "Winnie's safety is too important." He turned to go back into the room to tell the attorneys.

"No. That's the last thing you're going to decide right now. If you declare you're done with the case, Andy gets released and you will have nothing to offer the Crypt-Takers to get them to release Winnie."

His mind cleared. "Trevor...Trevor said he was trying to keep us safe. He said don't mess with *these* people. It's possible he's not one of them."

Delaney paced in front of him. "The CryptTakers might have something hanging over him. Maybe he wanted to track you to keep you safe, but the Crypt-Takers found his tracker." She spun to face him, her index finger pointing at his chest. "So that *was* him you spotted at the gas station."

"If he was stupid enough to get involved with a murderous organization then why would I trust him to keep my daughter safe? I can't let any of them get near Winnie." Something was gnawing at him, as if trying to connect a shorted wire in his brain. He just needed one minute of silence to grab onto the thought that seemed to have slipped away.

If his stepbrother had gotten involved with the hacking organization, it would likely be to pay off debts or to earn a big score. But how would Trevor have known about the security guard's death in time to plant the trackers in Winnie's shoes?

The puzzle pieces started snapping together at such a rapid pace, he struggled to keep up. "Hear me out and see if this makes sense. Trevor hired Andy just before he quit our business to leave for the Caribbean. I caught Andy trying to upload an update to the banks that would open up a back door for the CryptTakers. But maybe Trevor never wanted to go to the Caribbean. Maybe the only reason Trevor left the company was so there would no chance he'd be incriminated in the plan. Trevor could tell Andy how to get in the building without alerting any security."

"I'm following you so far."

His eyes widened. "Trevor said to let him fix it. He said everything would be fine by tomorrow."

"Because Andy will be released?"

He shook his head. "I don't think that's what he meant. The CryptTakers only do things for profit, right? They take orders from equally dangerous people who demand results." He looked directly at Delaney. "I think he's trying again."

"To hack into the bank systems?"

"It's a little more complicated than that. While Nancy and I waited for police in the server room, I programmed security measures to make sure no one could attempt what Andy did without first going into the server room and setting up administrative protocols."

"Which only you can do?"

His gut twisted. "Not just me—I wasn't the only one set up with access. I should have shut down his credentials when I bought him out, but when Trevor left, I'd hoped he would come back. At first I was going to give him two weeks, then a month… I didn't think the Caribbean would last. Time slipped by and I sort of forgot."

Delaney straightened. "You didn't revoke his security privileges."

"It started as a family firm. I planned on keeping it that way." The defensiveness rose above the shame for the briefest moment before his head cleared. "Trevor said to let him fix it. Maybe that means he's there now—alone with Winnie."

"Which means we might have a chance to get to her before the CryptTakers can." Delaney turned on her heel. "Are you coming?"

She didn't need to ask twice. He pumped his arms and ran alongside her to the door they'd first entered. She slowed and pointed at Bradford, who was speaking with the court security officers. "I need a tactical team at Bruce's company now. Tell them to come in silently and wait for my command when they get there."

"And contact the security company I contracted," Bruce added. "They should have some guards in my building right now."

Bradford threw the keys up in the air. "Take my ride."

Delaney snagged them and ran out the door. Four court security officers jogged alongside them, guns at the ready, eyes roaming the area.

"Which one is his car?"

She pointed at a silver vehicle. "The brand-new Charger."

Adrenaline pumped through his veins. He needed to get to Winnie as fast as possible or his heart would burst out of his chest. "I'm driving."

"Not happening." She threw open the driver's-side door and met his eyes across the top of the car. "I think you want someone who can legally speed."

"Good point." He jumped into the car and she threw it into gear before he'd put his seat belt on. The security guard had already opened the gate and before Bruce could regain his breath, Delaney had not only merged onto the freeway, she was swerving around vehicles while the speedometer kept rising.

"I'm suddenly very thankful they widened this freeway." She glanced at him. "Hold on." They reached a stretch of road with little traffic and the car released a growl that matched the intensity of his emotions. "Let's see how long it can stay over two hundred miles per hour."

"We're going to get her back." Bruce said it aloud. He needed to hear the words for himself.

"There's no doubt," she answered.

"If we go into WITSEC, I'll ask to include you, if you want. For Winnie's sake." Winnie deserved a mother. Whatever happened between him and Delaney didn't matter. All that mattered was the well-being of his sweet baby girl.

She bit her lip and squeezed the wheel tighter. "No offense, Bruce, but I need every single brain cell focused on driving right now."

"Of course." Though if she really wanted to be with them, why would that have taken any thought? Wouldn't she have answered yes right away? Maybe she only wanted to be with Winnie on her terms. The negative thoughts started to spiral, and he forced his eyes closed. *Help.* The single-word prayer was all he needed to clear his mind.

What was normally a forty-minute drive took a total of fifteen minutes. She pulled into the parking lot and dropped her speed down to a crawl as they drove around the office building. Three parked cars sat side by side close to the front entrance. Each one of them had the security company logo on the side. "If you're sure those are official cars, then there's no sign of anyone else here at all."

Bruce scanned the landscape. "Look." He pointed. "The truck is hidden in the trees. Sure looks like the same one we saw at the gas station."

She squinted. "Let's check it first and make sure he didn't leave Winnie there."

The junker contained a car seat but no Winnie. Delaney checked the ammunition in her weapon. "You should know I gave my two weeks' notice before we left."

He did a double take as they crept through the trees to approach the back door. "What? Why are you telling me this?"

"Because you should know I will break any rules I need to get Winnie back to you safely."

SIXTEEN

Delaney made sure she turned the volume on the radio attached to her waist to low. The team was five minutes out, but as Bruce had predicted, it seemed that only Trevor and Winnie were on-site.

"While I didn't revoke Trevor's security privileges on the network, he isn't listed as an acceptable visitor to the building during off hours. The security guys should've notified police by now if he's inside."

"Except Andy was able to sneak in without alerting your guard—using Trevor's know-how."

"True."

Bruce typed in his security clearance and the door popped open. She went through first, weapon raised. A security guard was on the ground. She bent down and felt for his pulse. Slower than she would like but strong enough to indicate that he'd been drugged.

Bruce's forehead tightened. "My brother did that?"

For someone that had been so sure of what his step-brother was and wasn't capable of, the surprise in his voice didn't offer comfort. To meet her daughter just to lose her again would destroy Delaney. She straightened and led Bruce down the hallway.

Around the corner, they discovered another guard down. His vitals were almost identical to the first. "Where do we go?" she asked.

Bruce pointed to the stairway door. "Server room. Trevor would need to gain admin access there before he could start the update process."

"You think he's doing the update personally? I thought you said he wasn't that good at hacking."

"He had to know this system backward and forward in order to sell it and answer questions with ease. I don't believe he could code a malware back door himself, but he wouldn't need to. He'd just need access to send whatever the CryptTakers gave him."

She kept her weapon up and her back against the stairway rail until they reached the basement floor. She reached for the door's handle.

"Stop."

She looked up the stairway in case he'd seen something. "What? What is it?"

"Last time I was down here, the CryptTakers killed someone. I don't want that to happen to you."

The concern in his voice warmed her heart. "Which is why you're going to let me go first so it doesn't happen to *you*."

"You don't know what to look for—you've never been here before. There are places they can hide in the cubicles, and there is another door down there."

She nodded. "I trained for shooters in office buildings, Bruce. Stay behind me and stay down."

He released a giant sigh but stopped arguing as they went through the door. Delaney realized he wasn't exaggerating. There were more hiding places in the room than any simulation she'd been in, but she didn't see any indication of his stepbrother. "Winnie?" she whispered.

Nothing.

Bruce tapped her shoulder. "To the left."

She stood next to the door of what had to be the server room as he put his hand on the access panel. The moment it clicked open she stuck her gun inside to look for Trevor. It was empty.

The server room reminded her of a panic room. Stepping past her, Bruce approached a keyboard that was attached to a wall of electronics that looked like blinking VCRs and DVD players to her untrained eye. She had a feeling not a single one could provide that kind of entertainment.

He tapped at the keys rapidly while studying the monitor and groaned.

"What's the problem?"

"He gained administrative access ten minutes ago. The update is halfway complete."

"Can you stop it?"

He nodded and typed a series of letters that looked like nonsense. "I can do better than that," he said. "I'm doing what I should've done a long time ago. I'm blocking Trevor's credentials." He hit Enter and gave her a side glance. "If he's somewhere in this building, he's going to know what happened—and he's going to come to us."

Delaney's radio crackled. She picked it up and heard the team's call sign. Help was on the premises. With Bruce's assistance, she provided them with the code needed to access the building. "One potentially armed man and small girl as a hostage on-site," she said into the radio.

"Are you good at negotiating hostage situations?" Bruce asked.

"I'm good at bringing in armed fugitives without hurting bystanders."

He blew out a breath. "I guess that's close enough."

It would have to be. She double-checked her weapon. "If you're right that Trevor is on the way, I want you to stay here and I'll wait outside for him."

"Not a chance."

"Bruce—"

"He's my brother. I want the chance to talk to him, to look him in the eye, before you take him down."

The way his jaw muscles worked made her doubt that he would give her the chance to do just that. "Let me be clear. If I see him, he will be cuffed before you have your chat. Let's go."

They didn't make it down the hallway before they heard the door on the opposite end of the room smack closed. A male voice muttered a string of curses as he stomped across the commercial-grade carpet.

Delaney crouched and aimed her weapon around the corner. "US Marshals. Hands up!"

"You've got to be kidding me." The man's voice sounded as smooth as butter. Despite knowing that Bruce and Trevor weren't blood relatives, she had formed a mental picture of Trevor that looked like Bruce. Instead, this man was a good five inches shorter, with thick jet-black hair that probably required an entire bottle of gel to hold it in its perfect S-shaped wave. His skin was tan and his eyes a light blue. He'd ditched the ball cap Bruce had seen the previous day and was wearing a crisp dress shirt, black dress pants and matching loafers as well as a silver watch that screamed money.

"There's obviously been a mistake. I work here. I'm an owner."

Trevor didn't have a visible weapon on his person, but more important, Winnie wasn't with him. If that scumbag had handed Winnie over to one of the Crypt-Takers, she'd—

"You sold out." Bruce stepped from behind her. Delaney tamped down her frustration at his interference. All that mattered was getting Winnie back, and in this instance, Bruce might know better how to handle his sibling. "In more ways than one."

Trevor's face crumpled. "You weren't supposed to come. Don't you ever listen to me?"

"Excuse me for not wanting my daughter to hang around with the CryptTakers."

Trevor narrowed his eyes. "Don't be petty. It doesn't suit you. You could've made real money. Everyone respects money more than ideals. You never got that, otherwise you'd still have Shannon."

Delaney reared back. Was he serious? Did this guy really think Bruce would want that kind of life? To essentially buy people's love? Even she knew him better than that, and she'd only known him for a few days.

Bruce shook his head. "Right now I could care less about what you do to my company. I only want Winnie."

"Relax. She's fine. She's in the building. Napping."

Bruce took a step closer. Delaney matched it, but she continued to train her gun on Trevor.

"How'd you find her?" Bruce asked. "We got rid of the trackers in the soles of her shoes."

Trevor at least had the courtesy to look ashamed. "The CryptTakers wanted your location. Zach insisted he have it—"

"Zach?"

Trevor reddened. "Doesn't matter who he is, just that he promised not to kill you if you cooperated. Which, of course, you didn't." His voice seethed with rage.

"Answer the question. How'd you find her after we got rid of the soles?"

"I was watching from a safe distance when I saw the cops put Andy in one cruiser. You and Nancy followed another cruiser. I knew then that you'd messed everything up. But, I also knew you'd have to be at the police station a long time. I went to your house and put the trackers in her shoes and her blanket."

Bruce reared back. "It was in her blanket?"

"But I checked her blanket." Delaney furrowed her brow.

"I couldn't be sure you'd take the right pair of shoes. I needed a backup."

"How could you do this to her?" Bruce took another step. "She's your niece! Does family mean nothing to you?"

"I was trying to keep you safe. Don't you get that?" Trevor snapped. "She'll be fine. She probably won't remember a thing."

Delaney's blood ran cold.

"What do you mean by that?" Bruce pressed.

"I gave her a little something. If she remembers anything, it'll be fuzzy, like a dream."

"You *drugged* her?" Bruce's fist flew out so fast, Delaney didn't have time to stop him. Trevor stumbled backward into the cubicle. Bruce grabbed either side of Trevor's pressed shirt. "Where is she?"

"Shannon has her, okay?"

Bruce's hands loosened and dropped his stepbrother, who slid down to the floor. "Shannon?"

Trevor rubbed his jaw. "She didn't like taking her the way we did, but it was necessary. She thought she would be able to keep Winnie calm if she woke up. We were going to bring her back right when it was done and Andy was released. So stop screwing things up."

"You and Shannon both joined the CryptTakers?"

He shrugged. "A couple years ago. The affair started a few months later." Trevor avoided looking him in the eye. "We didn't mean for it to happen. It just did."

Delaney's stomach churned at the look on Bruce's face. He hadn't had any idea that his wife had left him for his stepbrother.

"Save me the sob story," a man's voice snarled from behind Delaney. "Don't even think about it, darling," he said as she started to spin. "Drop the weapon."

Bruce turned in time to see Delaney bend over and set down her weapon. The gun rested halfway between her and Bruce but not close enough that he could lunge for it without getting shot himself.

"There's no need for guns, Zach," Trevor said as he straightened out his crumpled shirt. "Why don't you just give them some of that happy stuff you gave the guards?"

Zach scowled as he released a disgusted sigh. "The guards didn't see either one of us, now, did they? Instead of the no-risk operation that you promised, I've got two more witnesses. I can't have that. I'm not joining Andy in jail."

"Don't be hasty," Trevor said. "We need him. He's the only one that can get us the access to the banks now." He nodded toward Delaney. "And besides, there are probably more of her type arriving soon. We could use her to our advantage."

Zach shook his head. "No. We're cutting our losses. You'll be my hostage, and when we get out of here, you can be sure the CryptTakers will give you all the credit for not getting the job done."

Trevor looked as if he was going to lose his lunch on his designer shoes. As much as Bruce wanted to throttle him, he didn't want his stepbrother to die. Besides, he needed to know where Shannon had taken Winnie before the CryptTakers came after her, as well.

Zach raised his gun and Bruce didn't have time to register that the weapon was aimed at his heart. Delaney leaped toward him. The crack of the bullet didn't reach his ears until Delaney's back slammed against his chest.

His arms instinctively went around her waist as she dropped like a dead weight, taking him to his knees on the ground with her. The gun now within reach, Bruce grabbed it with his left hand.

Seeing the murderous look in the man's eyes, Bruce didn't take the time to aim properly and just pressed the trigger. The gun kicked back.

Zach's right shoulder flung backward and he bellowed as his shirt reddened.

Doors on either side of the floor slammed open. "US Marshals. Drop your weapons!"

Bruce let the gun fall to the ground as agents covered in tactical gear rushed in from all directions, rifles up. They surrounded Zach, shouting orders to get on the ground, despite his bloodied shoulder.

Delaney's head rested in the crook of Bruce's right arm, her eyes wide, her face panicked. A choking sound came from her mouth, followed by a huge gasp. She began coughing and groaning.

"Help me," Bruce called out. He looked down at her stomach where her hands were clutched. He carefully moved her hands away. She cringed, but he didn't see any blood. Instead he felt hard material underneath.

A deputy dropped to his knees. "Are you wearing a concealed vest?"

Delaney nodded, still coughing.

The deputy pulled up her shirt just enough to see the black material and a bullet embedded in the fabric. He ripped off the quick-release fastener on the left and winced.

"What? What is it?" Bruce's heart pounded fast.

Delaney sucked in another breath. "He's trying not to tell me I'm going to need stitches."

"A lot of stitches, and you'll end up with the nastiest bruise you've ever seen. You should be grateful that's all you'll need, wearing such a thin vest and taking a bullet at such close range," the deputy said. "If the shooter had used a 9 mm instead of the .45 Magnum, I doubt this thing would've stopped it. The plate bent the bullet enough so that only the tip injured her."

She groaned. "Still felt like I was hit with a hammer."

He pulled out a first-aid kit the size of a pack of index cards from one of seven pockets lining his pants legs. "Get the vest off of her."

Delaney pointed toward her right shoulder. Bruce found and unlatched the fasteners on either side. The deputy pulled the vest away while leaving her shirt on top.

"If the bullet had gone any deeper, you'd probably need surgery." He pursed his lips. "It looks like a puncture wound to me but only flesh deep. You should feel better without that sticking into you." The deputy attached thick gauze and tape, and pressed the bandage against her abdomen before pulling her shirt back over it. "Keep pressure on it. You'll definitely need it checked out. I'm not a medic." He rose. "An ambulance is on the way."

"Help me up," she said to Bruce.

"Are you sure?"

"Of course, I'm sure."

He cradled her in his arms and lifted her to stand. His thoughts were muddled as he tried to sort out what had just happened. He turned to the deputies who had handcuffed Trevor. "Where's Winnie?"

Trevor's eyes and mouth were clamped shut.

"Trevor! Where is she?"

He groaned. "With Shannon, like I told you."

"Where?"

Delaney stepped forward. Her hand was still on her stomach, which should have made her look fragile, but when the other deputies saw the look on her face, they stepped to the side. She tilted her head and stared at him until Trevor lifted his eyes to meet hers. "See," she said, in a soft but firm voice, "if you think not telling us where to find Winnie gives Shannon a chance to escape, you're wrong. If you think she could survive on the run from both the CryptTakers and me, you're wrong, as well. I can guarantee you that I will do my part to leave no stone unturned to find my daughter."

Trevor's eyes widened. "Your—" He glanced at Bruce and could clearly see the truth all over his face as his shoulders sagged. "They're holed up in Bruce's office on the third floor. Knock three times or Shannon's supposed to come out blazing."

"What? What do you mean blazing?"

"She wouldn't hurt Winnie. You know her."

"Do I?" Bruce bellowed.

The deputy closest to Bruce picked up his radio and issued a command that no one approach any closed doors on the third floor without prior approval. "Thanks," Delaney said.

"I need to see her right away."

She nodded. "I wouldn't make you wait. We'll go up and have the deputies escort us in after the three knocks."

Bruce led her to the elevator. He was in a hurry, but he wasn't about to make the woman who took a bullet for him go up the stairs. They stepped through the steel doors.

"Are you okay?" she asked.

He reared back. "Me?" Bruce couldn't fathom why she was worried about him. "I want to throttle my brother and ex-wife, but as long as Winnie is safe and sound, that's what matters."

"What Trevor said—"

It dawned on him that she meant the news about Shannon's affair with his stepbrother. He offered her a small smile. "It hurt to know, but as soon as he said it I realized it didn't surprise me." What did surprise him was that Delaney cared enough to ask. He sighed. "In many ways they're made for each other." He couldn't take his eyes off Delaney as the elevator ascended. "Why'd you do that? Jump in front of me?"

She blinked slowly, and then a small smile spread across her face. "What was I supposed to do? Let them try to kill you?" She parroted the words he'd spoken to her once.

He tried to match her smile, but he couldn't. If he had lost her… He drew in a breath. His bones burned hot with shame for even imagining Delaney would lie to him or manipulate him to get to Winnie. She was not like Shannon or Trevor. This woman didn't belittle integrity. She sought it. She wanted to please the Lord, as he did. They both made mistakes, but they both wanted to get up and do the next right thing. What if they were made for each other? Could she ever entertain the idea?

Her expression sobered. "I couldn't let you die."

"Don't tell me it's your job."

"Well, it is, but I did it also because…" She worried her lip and turned away.

The unsaid words hung in the air. Bruce couldn't think for a second. He loved her. He did.

Did she?

"I…I couldn't let Winnie's father die." She said meekly. "But…"

"I love you." The words came out of his mouth before he could stop them. Deep down he wanted to know her feelings before he put his own out there, on the chance she would stomp them or use them to her advantage, but the woman in front of him didn't use words flippantly. Actions meant something to her.

She blinked rapidly. "I love you, too." The words came out in a whisper. The elevator dinged and the doors opened. With one hand pressed against her abdomen and the other hand holding her gun, she pulled her shoulders back. "Point me to your office, then stay back."

SEVENTEEN

Delaney had never appreciated her training more than at this moment because without that practice she never would've been able to corral the hundreds of thoughts and feelings begging for attention. She shoved them aside to deal with later, after she knew Winnie was safe.

Bruce frowned. "If Shannon sees me first, it's less likely she'll shoot."

Delaney wanted to argue, but given his history and Trevor's admission that Shannon hadn't wanted any part in kidnapping Winnie in the first place, she weighed it against her own plan. "We'll compromise, then."

She gestured for two deputies to follow them. Her stomach burned with hot pain. Grandpa had insisted she wear what used to be her grandma's concealable vest. It was much thinner than the ballistic vest she normally wore during a raid, but it had done the job. Mostly. "You'll stand behind me."

"And risk you getting shot again? No." He noted her determined face and pointed to one of the other deputies. "What about him? He has on a tactical vest."

The deputy looked at them with one eyebrow raised but didn't comment.

If Delaney hadn't already declared her resignation in two weeks, she would've been embarrassed that a citizen was openly worried for her safety. She stepped forward to the wooden door Bruce had indicated and knocked three times, then stepped to the right side, effectively blocking Bruce. One deputy stood at an angle to her and the other stood on the opposite side of the door.

The doorknob turned and swung open. A petite blonde woman stood behind the door. "Trev—" Her mouth gaped open as the deputy in front charged and pulled her arms behind her back in a split second. Shannon looked past Delaney. "Bruce?" Her voice wobbled.

"Where is she?" Bruce said.

Delaney took one step into the office. In the opposite corner, her sweet little girl slept, curled up with Lovey. She ran to Winnie but stopped herself from picking up the little girl. She turned to Bruce. "She'll want her dad when she wakes up."

Bruce dropped to one knee and felt for her pulse. Delaney took comfort in Winnie's soft, rhythmic breathing and the way her long lashes fluttered ever so slightly against her cheeks.

"She should wake up soon," Shannon said softly.

They both turned to her at the same time.

Bruce stood. "What'd you give her?"

"I'm sorry, Bruce," Shannon said. "I didn't want to be a part of this. We never wanted to hurt you. Trevor insisted your business wouldn't even be hurt, that you would never have to know." She lifted her chin. "It's always been Trevor. I didn't think he had any interest in me, but when I found out he always had, I—"

Bruce's eyes bulged in a look of disbelief. "Just tell me what you gave her."

Shannon looked flustered but not a single hair fell from her updo. "I don't know. It was a small dose of whatever they gave the security guards. Trevor measured it and gave her the shot. She's supposed to wake up soon."

The radios crackled with news of an ambulance on the scene. Delaney turned to the closest deputy. "Please ask the paramedics to come here."

The other deputy shoved Shannon out of the room, reciting her Miranda rights. "Wait," Delaney called. She walked to the doorway and aimed her question at Shannon. "Where's the tracker?"

Shannon glanced around as if fearing someone would overhear. "Underneath the embroidered puppy." The deputy moved Shannon to the elevator, leaving Delaney speechless. She turned around. "How could it be underneath the puppy? That's so small."

Bruce was a step ahead of her. He grabbed a pair of scissors from his desk and carefully cut a few stitches of the seam on the Lovey. It was enough for his finger to get in between the two pieces of fabric and slide underneath the faded blue puppy. Judging by his expression, he'd found it. He pulled out what looked like a sticker. "The smallest GPS tracker on the market." He shook his head and handed it to her. "I don't know how I'm going to forgive them."

"You have to make the choice to forgive, but you also need to give all your hurt to God. Sometimes hourly." She sighed and glanced down at her beautiful daughter. "I should know. I had to forgive myself for…"

She couldn't even say it. The only sound remaining

in the room was that of Winnie breathing. Bruce stood up and crossed the room.

Her stomach grew hotter, but Delaney didn't think it was due to the flesh wound. All the thoughts and feelings she'd shoved aside came rushing back. She'd admitted her love for Bruce. Had she imagined that he'd proclaimed his love for her? Did the moment with Shannon or the reminder of Delaney's past change things?

Bruce wiped away a tear that was on her right cheek. His fingers were soft as they slid gently down her face and around the back of her neck. "I love you, Delaney." He leaned over and kissed her so softly and yet so fully that she lost her balance. His other hand caught the small of her back and kept her upright just as the paramedics entered the room. She winked at him. "Don't get a big head, thinking you've knocked me off my feet. It's just because I was shot."

A twinkle appeared in his eye. "I really hope we get to test your theory after you're all patched up."

Movement on the couch caught her attention. Winnie was upright with her thumb in her mouth. "Why do you have my Lovey, Daddy?"

A strangled laugh escaped him. He picked up Winnie in his arms and kissed her forehead. Winnie scrunched up her nose and looked at Delaney. "Why is Daddy crying?" Her eyes widened. "'Cuz he doesn't have a Lovey?"

"I'm pretty sure you are his Lovey," Delaney answered, her heart beating hard against her chest.

Bruce beamed and turned to her, his smile fading. "Are you okay? You're turning pale."

She had a hard time processing his words. She wanted to tell Winnie right then just how much she loved her as well, but it wasn't the right time. She hadn't even had the conversation with Bruce about it, and she didn't want to rush things.

Besides, he still had a trial to testify in, and the need for WITSEC hadn't been ruled out as of yet.

Her head began to spin. A paramedic asked her to sit down as Winnie pointed to Delaney's hand, still putting pressure against her wound. Blood seeped past her fingers.

"Did you get an owie?" Winnie's face blurred and everything went black.

Bruce paced the court hallway. Three days had passed and he'd still not been allowed to see or contact Delaney. It was driving him mad despite news that she was recovering. The deputy he'd suggested be his human shield at the office building had taken over his protective detail until Andy's trial, which had been rescheduled, given the "extenuating circumstances," to today.

He'd done it. He'd finally testified.

Two court security officers flanked Bruce until Marshal Bradford exited through the tall wooden doors. "They're sentencing him right now." Bradford placed a hand on his shoulder. "You did well."

Bruce gaped. "I thought the prosecutor wanted to give him a deal so he'd give up the CryptTakers."

"The US Attorney didn't tell you?" Bradford smiled. "They didn't need to offer a deal. Justice will be served for Max's death. The US Attorney had two individuals affiliated with the CryptTakers who hadn't committed murder who were able to hand down every detail they had learned from the past two years in exchange for WITSEC. You are officially a free man."

"Two individuals, huh? Do I happen to know them?"

"I can't comment specifically, but you might."

Bruce nodded. "I hope they'll be happy together." He surprised himself by actually meaning it. As Delaney had suggested, once he'd made the choice, forgiveness started to come easier. He was human, though, and the knowledge that he'd never have to see them again helped more than he wanted to admit. "So I can go home now?"

"One second. I need to page the deputy who is watching Winnie."

The doors at the end of the hall burst open and Winnie, laughing, ran down the hallway toward Bruce. A gorgeous brunette with her hair down echoed her laugh, jogging at a slow pace behind her.

He'd never seen Delaney with her hair down. The way she looked matched how he felt—free. Her smile wide, her eyes lit, she was beautiful.

"Is she going to catch me, Daddy?" Winnie darted a quick glance over her shoulder and squealed.

Bruce got down on one knee and placed a finger over his mouth in case the people inside the courtroom could hear. She vaulted into his arms and he picked her up. Delaney slowed to a stop, but her smile didn't fade.

Bruce glanced at her stomach. "Are you okay? Should you really be running? They wouldn't let me see you at the hospital."

Marshal Bradford chuckled. "I think she'll be fine. It's her last day here. Delaney, your last assignment is to take them home."

Her professional exterior snapped into place. "Yes, sir."

Bradford winked and turned to walk away. "I'll let you catch up."

Delaney relaxed again, and Bruce wanted to do whatever it took to keep that relaxed, at-peace smile on her face…for as long as they both shall live. He stepped forward.

"I thought you had given two weeks' notice. Today is your last day?"

Her cheeks looked rosy. "Given the injury, Bradford suggested I go ahead and leave. I have a ridiculous amount of sick time and vacation days built up. I can take my time finding another job."

"Perhaps in forensics, a field you actually want to work in?"

Her eyes warmed. "Perhaps."

"Are you fully healed?"

"I'm a little sore from the impact and all the stitches, but I'm okay. I lost more blood than I'd realized at first, but the bullet didn't penetrate any organs. It was a bad puncture wound, but it could've been much, much worse."

"I owe your grandpa a big thank-you card for making you wear that vest."

"I think he'd prefer you thank him in person by coming to dinner sometime." She looked down and seemed shy all of a sudden. "I mean, if you want to. I'm…I'm staying with them until I get my own place in Ames."

He stepped closer to her and reached for her hand. "I would *love* to." He emphasized the word for Delaney's sake without spelling it out in front of Winnie, a reminder that his feelings hadn't changed a single bit. He knew they had a lot to sort out about how to handle the transition to Delaney being in Winnie's life, but for Bruce's part, he'd never felt so confident that pursuing Delaney was the right thing.

She eyed him. "Well, I would *love* to give you two a ride home."

His heart beat faster. He glanced at Winnie. "Ready to go home?"

Her eyes widened in the same way Delaney's did. "To *our* home?"

"Yes."

"With *my* toys? And *my* bed? And—"

Bruce nodded as he laughed and set Winnie down. "Let's see if you can race us to that door down there."

She giggled and took off. Bruce couldn't resist catching Delaney before she started running, as well. He pulled her close and kissed her. "I missed you. I can't wait to spend time with you."

"Me, too."

"Hey, guys." Winnie had turned around and had her hands on her hips. "Catch up."

Delaney smiled. "She doesn't need to ask me twice."

They ran together toward the door, and Bruce couldn't help but pray that they were also running toward a future together.

EPILOGUE

Two Months Later

Delaney honestly couldn't remember when she'd had so much fun. Every day of the past two months seemed to top the last. And today was Winnie's birthday. She'd initially balked when Bruce had suggested they take in a football game together—without Winnie.

"Are you kidding? It's her birthday." It especially surprised her since he'd been the one who had once told her that it seemed selfish to watch football when he could be spending time with his daughter.

He held her hand. "Yes, but we're both learning to enjoy life. And your parents and grandparents would love the chance to spend some time spoiling her on her birthday."

That softened her. "Of course they would."

"So I suggested they get that time while I take you out on a date so we could cheer for our alma mater. We can meet them afterward and do cake and presents together."

Joy washed over her so intensely, her breath caught.

"You know," Bruce said as he bent down so she could

stare right into his green eyes. "Maybe it's time for you to tell her."

"I'm...I'm not sure yet." Bruce had been encouraging her for the last week to tell Winnie that she was her mom.

"She would be thrilled," he insisted.

Deep down Delaney wanted nothing more than to share the news. Her parents and grandparents already knew, of course, but they respected that Bruce was Winnie's father and didn't want to cross any lines. Now Bruce was leaving the decision up to Delaney, and it terrified her.

"Things are going so well with us," she said. She struggled to find the right words. "I don't want you to feel undue pressure if I tell her. I can wait."

His eyes softened. "Are you worried that I might reject you or that Winnie might reject you?"

Busted. She worried her lip. "Do I have to answer?"

He laughed. "So it's both. Well, since I know better than most that actions mean more than words, I say you need a fun date with yours truly without having to think about anything other than your job interview on Monday."

"Oh, thanks for that. Now I'm thinking about Monday."

He laughed. "We both know it's just a formality."

She rolled her eyes for his benefit, though he had a point. She'd been told the entry-level forensics position was hers if she wanted it. After so many years of holding on to hurt and worry so tightly, it was hard to grab hope and love and joy without feeling guilty. She remembered her grandma's words once more. If she could accept the biggest gift of all from God's love, then surely she could accept the smaller gifts in life, as well. "Let's go watch some football."

Three hours later, her mouth hurt from smiling so much. Bruce had held her hand during every moment of the game except when they'd jumped in the stands, pumping their fists with the other alumni. The Cyclones and Hawkeyes were neck and neck, but their team scored a touchdown in the last two minutes.

They took their time filing out of the stadium. She'd never been more relaxed in her life. Bruce glanced at his phone. "Your family took Winnie to Reiman Gardens. Mind if we join them there?"

"Of course not. We're practically there already." Delaney had a bounce to her step she couldn't recall ever having before. "I have Winnie's birthday present in the car."

"Let's save that for cake, if you don't mind, and walk over. My legs could do with a stretch."

Ten minutes later they entered the remarkably quiet gardens. The stark contrast to the chaos of the game was welcome, though, as she inhaled the floral scents. "The last time we were here together, we didn't really get to enjoy it."

He pointed down a path she didn't recall. "I'd like to show you one of my favorite walks. I used to take this path a lot when I needed to think, pray and make big decisions."

A sign on the right said Closed for Private Party. She groaned. "Sorry. Maybe we can come back another time."

He stood on his tiptoes and looked out past the sign. "I'm sure whatever's going on hasn't started yet, and this won't take long."

She folded her arms. "Since when is Bruce Walker a rule breaker?"

He grinned. "I promise I'll leave if asked." He took her hand and pulled her underneath a rose-covered trellis. A podium stood in the center with an intricately cut crystal vase that held a single red rose. The sun streamed through the various grooves of the vase, projecting a dazzling prism of colors all around them. "It's so beautiful."

Bruce regarded it. "The rose looks different than the rest of the roses on the trellis. I wonder if it smells different."

She felt her left eyebrow rise. His comment seemed odd. Bruce's eyebrows and mouth twitched as if he was fighting off a smile. He lost the battle as he laughed and shrugged. "Just a thought to consider."

Delaney humored him and walked over to smell it, but when she leaned over she saw that in the center of the rose rested a beautiful diamond ring. She fought back a gasp, but her heart sped up. She dared not assume. She straightened.

He tilted his head. "You didn't smell it."

"Someone's planning to propose here, Bruce."

He nodded slowly and gulped, all humor gone from his face. He picked up the vase, bent down on one knee and gently held her fingers with his other hand. "Delaney Elizabeth Patton, I fell in love with your integrity, your beauty, your compassion…"

She blinked rapidly, trying to see him clearly through the sheen of tears. Her throat closed so tight she feared she might not be able to breathe again. She'd never been loved and cherished in this way, never imagined it could be possible. She laughed as he continued to list things he loved about her. "Bruce, am I going to get a chance to list the things I love about *you*?"

He shook his head. "Only if you say yes." He held up the vase higher. "Will you marry me?"

She bent over and kissed him firmly on the mouth, then pulled back just an inch. "Yes," she whispered.

He set down the vase and slipped the ring onto her finger before he stood up and wrapped his arms around her. "Now, about those things you love about me…"

She kissed him again, a gesture of love she would never grow tired of. "I'm thinking we'll write our own vows so you can hear them at our wedding."

He pulled his chin back. "No fair. I've already used my best material. Although I could talk about how you saved our lives."

"In many ways, I feel like you saved my life." She froze as she heard a familiar giggle in the distance. "Are we really meeting Winnie here?"

"Yes." He pressed his lips together and held both her hands. "I know this day was the hardest day of your life three years ago. I know I can't erase those memories, but I'm hoping we can give you good ones from now on."

His thoughtfulness overwhelmed her. Three years ago at this time of day, she'd been sobbing in a hospital, losing what she thought had been her last chance at love, at family. Bruce turned and led her past the rest of the rose garden, following the sound of bells and laughter.

Her parents, grandparents, and Stephen and Kathy Bradford stood around Winnie, who danced on metallic squares that produced the ringing chimes. They looked up expectantly at Bruce and Delaney.

Delaney held up her hand and they cheered.

Winnie, obviously thinking they were cheering for her, kept dancing. "Mommy, Daddy, watch me!"

The group collectively held their breath. Delaney glanced at Bruce. "Did you tell her?"

He shook his head, tears filling his eyes, as well. "No."

Her heart nearly burst. She stood up on her tiptoes and kissed him before taking his hand. She turned to face Winnie, shedding her fear and worry, and ready to accept her new life with nothing but thankfulness. "We're ready, sweetie. Mommy and Daddy are here."

* * * * *

If you loved this story,
don't miss these other heart-stopping romances
by Heather Woodhaven:

Countdown
Texas Takedown
Tracking Secrets
Credible Threat

Find these and other great reads at
www.LoveInspired.com

Dear Reader,

This was probably the hardest story for me to write thus far, though perhaps I think that of every book I've just finished.

During the writing of this book, my son's recovery from a routine surgery became a nightmare. For a brief moment, I thought we'd lost him. I'll never forget that night, and I'm abundantly thankful for the doctor who wasn't even supposed to still be there and the on call surgery team that arrived impossibly fast during rush hour. After two weeks of little sleep, my son fully recovered and is doing better than ever.

Toward the end of writing, my sweet dog, and the inspiration for *Tracking Secrets*, collapsed in the living room and took her last breath. She'd been by my side for the past eleven years, usually trying to put her head on top of the laptop while I typed or flopping on my feet so I had no choice but to keep writing. I'm thankful I have nothing but fond and hilarious memories of her. She was the ideal dog for our family.

So my emotional rollercoaster may have seeped through the pages of the book. It served as a reminder that if you haven't experienced some things yourself, you might not understand. Even with research. My apologies if I portrayed any aspect of the adoption journey incorrectly as I haven't been part of an adoption personally.

Delaney's journey compelled me. She could accept God's forgiveness but had a harder time forgiving herself. I think everyone battles the tendency to some extent. Winnie has similar traits to my youngest and a certain precocious niece. She was a delight to write. And finally, Iowa is an amazing place to grow up. I'm glad I was able to set the story there. I hope to visit again soon.

Blessings,
Heather Woodhaven

Get 4 FREE REWARDS!

We'll send you 2 FREE Books plus 2 FREE Mystery Gifts.

Love Inspired® Suspense books feature Christian characters facing challenges to their faith... and lives.

FREE Value Over **$20**

SPECIAL EXCERPT FROM

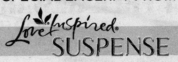

*A reporter enlists the help of a soldier and his
bomb-sniffing dog to stay one step ahead of the
bomber who wants her dead.*

Read on for a sneak preview of
Explosive Force *by Lynette Eason,*
the next book in the Military K-9 Unit miniseries,
available September 2018 from Love Inspired Suspense.

First Lieutenant Heidi Jenks, news reporter for CAF News,
blew a lock of hair out of her eyes and did her best to keep
from muttering under her breath about the boring stories
she was being assigned lately.

Heidi shut the door to the church where her interviewee
had insisted on meeting and walked down the steps. She
shivered and glanced over her shoulder. For some reason
she expected to see Boyd Sullivan, as if the fact that she
was alone in the dark would automatically mean the serial
killer was behind her.

After being chased by law enforcement last week, he'd
fallen from a bluff and was thought to be dead. But when
his body was never found, that assumption changed. He
was alive. Somewhere.

Heidi's steps took her past the base hospital. She was
getting ready to turn onto the street that would take her

home when a flash of movement from the K-9 training center caught her eye. Her steps slowed, and she heard a door slam.

A figure wearing a dark hoodie bolted down the steps and shot off toward the woods behind the center. He reached up, shoved the hoodie away and yanked something—a ski mask?—off his head then pulled the hoodie back up. He stuffed the ski mask into his jacket pocket.

Very weird actions that set Heidi's internal alarm bells screaming. She decided it was prudent to get out of sight.

Just as she moved to do so, the man spun.

And came to an abrupt halt as his eyes locked on hers.

Ice invaded her veins. He took a step toward her then shot a look back at the training center. With one last threatening glare, he whirled and raced toward the woods once again.

Like he wanted to put as much distance between him and the building as possible.

Don't miss
Explosive Force *by Lynette Eason,*
available September 2018 wherever
Love Inspired® Suspense books and ebooks are sold.

www.LoveInspired.com

Looking for inspiration in tales
of hope, faith and heartfelt romance?

Check out **Love Inspired®** and
Love Inspired® Suspense books!

New books available every month!

CONNECT WITH US AT:

Harlequin.com/Community

Facebook.com/HarlequinBooks

Twitter.com/HarlequinBooks

Instagram.com/HarlequinBooks

Pinterest.com/HarlequinBooks

ReaderService.com

LIGENRE2018